ALL MY DANGEROUS FRIENDS

By the same author

Trouble All the Way

Sparkle and Nightflower

The Glass House

Wilful Blue

Sleeping Dogs

The Devil Latch

Black Foxes

Princes

Sonya
HARTNETT

ALL MY DANGEROUS FRIENDS

VIKING

Viking
Penguin Books Australia Ltd
487 Maroondah Highway, PO Box 257
Ringwood, Victoria 3134, Australia
Penguin Books Ltd
Harmondsworth, Middlesex, England
Penguin Putnam Inc.
375 Hudson Street, New York, New York 10014, USA
Penguin Books Canada Limited
10 Alcorn Avenue, Toronto, Ontario, Canada, M4V 3B2
Penguin Books (N.Z.) Ltd
Cnr Rosedale and Airborne Roads, Albany, Auckland, New Zealand
Penguin Books (South Africa) (Pty) Ltd
4 Pallinghurst Road, Parktown 2193, South Africa

First published by Penguin Books Australia, 1998
10 9 8 7 6 5 4 3 2 1

Cover design by Nikki Townsend, Penguin Design Studio
Typeset in 11.5/18 Weiss and 10.5/18 ITC Legacy Sans Medium
Made and printed in Australia by Australian Print Group, Maryborough, Victoria

National Library of Australia
Cataloguing-in-Publication data:

Hartnett, Sonya, 1968– .
All my dangerous friends.

ISBN 0 670 88027 2.

I. Title.

A823.3

For Erica Irving

With thanks to John

The first time I met him wasn't the first time I had seen him. Eager to say anything that might blunt the awkwardness of being there, of meeting a stranger, of wanting to please when I didn't know what was considered pleasant, I jabbed a finger towards his face and burst out to him, 'Oh, I've seen you before!'

Sasha Johns did not flinch; he looked at me without recognition but with a kind of noncommitted kindness, as at a simpleton. 'Really,' he said.

'On a train, once. With a blind man.'

The smallest frown dived down Sasha's face and he glanced at Andy. We were outside in a beer garden because it was a mild night, the last mild night that autumn would sneak from winter that year, as if the sullen season had looked elsewhere for a moment, and Andy seemed to sink deeper into the shade. Sasha switched his sights to me, said, 'I don't think it was me.'

'Well it was someone who looked exactly like you – '

'Sasha would maybe remember being on a train with a blind man,' suggested Andy. I shook my head, my hands gripping the table's edge.

'It was with a blind man,' I insisted hopelessly, wishing back the words, wishing myself away. The two of them were staring and I sagged against the arm of my chair, dazed by my own gracelessness.

'I'll go to the bar,' Andy announced, and pushed out his chair. My heart sank to be left alone but there was nothing that might be done, nothing that could be said, to make anything any worse. Sasha watched him disappear into the crowd before looking at me and smiling grimly. After a moment he said, 'I don't go much on the trains.'

I waved a hand lankly. 'I thought it was you.'

'I don't know anyone blind.'

'No,' I sighed, 'he wasn't your friend.'

I fell into blissful muteness; Sasha propped on an elbow. The people in the beer garden formed a loose circle around our table, friends clustered with other friends and all of them with much to talk about, much to make them laugh. Sasha coughed lightly, clearing his throat. He tilted his glass, which was empty, and peered into it. As if there was inspiration in its depths he asked abruptly, 'How old are you?'

'. . . Eighteen.'

'Just a baby. You don't have to impress me.'

It made me lift my gaze. Sasha was handsome, his eyes in the shade of great long lashes and his mop of hair in hooks around his coat's collar, but I remember wishing we had never met. 'I'm not trying to impress you.'

'Then why are you so nervous?'

I pouted crossly, my face hot. 'Wouldn't you be?'

'Maybe,' he said.

It made me smile, reluctantly. 'I'm nearly nineteen,' I told him. 'Two more months.'

'Don't wish your life away,' he said. He looked around the garden, at the ratty azaleas growing from their bed of tanbark and cigarette ash, and then he looked at the table, at the knots in the slats of greeny pine and at the butts he had crushed while waiting for us to arrive. 'What were you doing on the train?'

'Nothing. Going to school.'

'You go to university with Andy?'

'Andy's in the year above me.'

Sasha nodded. Andy was twenty-three, an age that seemed infinitely world-wise to me, and one I couldn't imagine reaching. I waited for Sasha to utter the words 'cradle' and 'snatching' and conclude with a smirk, but instead he asked, 'Is your studying going well?'

'I don't want to talk about school,' I replied, rashly. 'It's what you talk about when there's nothing else to say.'

'All right, what do you want to talk about?'

There was a moment of silence between us, silence that made itself loud and conspicuous despite the music and the noise. 'University,' I said, 'is harder than I thought it would be.'

'I see. You're going to drop out, then?'

'No. I like it.'

'But if you are not smart enough . . .'

'I'll make myself smart,' I said. 'I'll do it. I'm not worried.'

He nodded. 'You don't like defeat.'

'Who does?' I asked.

'Not me,' he replied.

We smiled at each other; Sasha sat back and linked his hands behind his head. I dabbed a finger to a bead of spilled beer and flicked off the drop that clung. 'It's terrible, discovering you're not as smart as you thought you were,' I said.

'I can imagine. Whatever made you think you were smart?'

'At school I used to get good marks.'

'Maybe you were only smart in comparison to the people you were at school with. Did you go to school with a crowd of morons?'

'I went to a private girls' school,' I said. 'Some of them were very smart. But you could be dumb if you didn't have a boyfriend, or you got your essays in on time, or you didn't wear the latest clothes.'

'Ah, so they *were* stupid.'

I smiled. Of course I had thought they were. 'They could be horrible, those girls,' I sighed. 'I was glad to finish school and get away from them.'

'You must have been lonely there. Long, lonely years.'

'I did have some friends,' I said hastily. 'I had a friend. I didn't hang around all by myself.'

'One friend?' Sasha cocked an eyebrow.

'And I knew it would end, that I'd eventually be free. That something better would come along.'

'A new life?'

'. . . I hope so.'

Sasha took a pack of cigarettes from his coat pocket and stripped off the plastic. 'A new life,' he said thoughtfully. 'You're smart and expensively educated and you have, for goodness sake, a little silver bracelet around your wrist. Someone has hopes for you. But you're sitting at a sticky table in a dingy beer garden, surrounded by alcohol and loud-mouthed strangers, spilling all your secrets to someone you hardly know. You're wearing new clothes, I think you bought them specially to wear tonight, but you went for appearance over comfort and now you are cold, though you will not complain. Your boyfriend took the first opportunity to abandon you, forcing you to struggle on alone. This boyfriend is an unkempt fellow, he doesn't brush his hair, his clothes are sadly tatty. He doesn't have any money, nor prospects to speak of. Somehow I suspect your parents would not approve of your new life. Cigarette?'

I took one and he sparked a flame in my face. 'I'm an oldest child,' I told him. 'It's my duty to do things my parents don't like.'

'That is an easy answer.'

I squinted at him through smoke and he looked back cagily. His skin was clear and coloured like sand, as if he'd recently returned from somewhere coastal and warm, but he would remain that way the whole time I knew him, and that was just the way he was. 'I've spent most of my life bored out of my mind,' I said. 'I've spent most of it killing time. All those years don't matter to me: I had to live them in order to get here, tonight. I always knew who I was, inside, I knew how I wanted to be. I'm just not very practised at being it yet.'

He considered this, his cigarette to his lips. 'Is Andy your first boyfriend?'

'He's not really my *boyfriend*. I hardly know him.'

'How did you meet him?'

'I told you, at uni.'

'But *how*,' he persisted. 'How?'

The music and the noise had been getting louder and by now we were straining to hear each other. 'Are you genuinely interested,' I asked, 'or just making conversation?'

'Making conversation, I suppose.'

I snorted. 'He's taking his time getting those beers.'

'I can see him from here. He's talking to someone.'

So I told Sasha the story, having nothing else to say. 'My mother would have been pleased, if she'd been there. Andy offered me a cup of tea.'

Sasha widened his eyes. 'How dashing,' he said.

'I'd been perving on him since the start of the year but he'd never once looked at me, and then one day I was just sitting in the common room minding my own business and he came in and started making a cup of tea, and he turned around and asked me if I wanted one. A cup of tea.'

'And so the romance was brewed. I'm sure he'll come back for you eventually, what with that background between yourselves.'

'Has he said anything about me?'

'Simply that he'd met you.'

'But what did he say?'

'He didn't say a thing. Would you like that, if he was discussing you with his friends?'

'I don't know,' I said. 'Maybe.'

'You wouldn't,' he assured me. He settled back in his chair and folded his arms. 'Andy is very kind,' he said. 'You'll never forget your first boyfriend, so Andy will be a good first boyfriend for you to have. He will set a high standard, so you will never settle for less than you should.'

'Sasha! Stop it.'

He chuckled, smoke coming out his nose; his teasing made me pinken with happiness. His eyes roamed: 'Your beau returns.'

Andy put down three glasses of beer and frowned. 'Were you talking about me?'

'No,' said Sasha. 'I was asking Louie if *Louie* is short for Louise.'

'It's not,' I said. 'It's only Louie.'

'Why? Did your parents want a boy?'

'No. They just liked the name. What about you? How come you're Sasha? Are your parents Russian?'

'No,' Sasha laughed, 'it's very sad, they wanted a dog.'

So that was how I met Sasha Johns and, through him, the rest. The night in the beer garden was the third time I had been out with Andy and the first time we'd gone out with company. I wanted his friends to like me and Andy wanted me to like his friends: it was no coincidence that Sasha was the first of them that I'd be invited to meet, and no less a coincidence that Andy should get caught up on his way to the bar and leave the two of us alone so long. Sasha had charm, and wits he could call upon to fill a gaping silence, but, more than that, Sasha was ringleader and mastermind. He was lying when he said I didn't need to impress him: impressing him was everything. Life would have become difficult for Andy if he had liked someone that Sasha did not. Sasha didn't, for instance, care for Hastings's girlfriend Elsbeth, and christened her with the nickname *Handbrake*, and soon everyone was calling her that, and composing strange songs about her, and Hastings was made to suffer. But Hastings's role was vital to the running of the business and he was treated more leniently than Andy could hope to be under similar scorn, for Andy was not indispensable. He wasn't there because they needed him, he was only there because his path had once crossed and linked with theirs. He shared years of history with them, but the business they operated was never a sentimental thing. He had the trust of his friends, but trust is cheap: you can buy trust with fear. They would have been disappointed to lose him, but friendships fizzle every day.

They needn't have worried. Had Andy been driven to choose, he would never have chosen me. And I don't blame him for that. I don't take it as a personal insult. I know it is more important to have friends than girlfriends.

It started to drizzle later in the evening and the three of us moved inside. The tables were all taken and we had to stand, guarding our glasses against elbows and gradually extending our tacky patch of carpet. Sasha and Andy knew people and these people would struggle through the crowd to reach us, and the conversation would be short and sharp, hacked down to essentials.

'How you doing Andy.'

'Good Tone. Yourself.'

'Good Andy. Sash.'

'Tone.'

'Things going well.'

'Yeah.'

The visitor to our circle would flash a glance at me, someone they didn't know.

'Hi. I'm Tony. How you doing.'

'Hello. I'm Louie.'

And the visitor would be lost for words, unable, in the presence of a stranger, to say the ones he'd hoped to. He'd swing his erratic attention to Sasha and say, 'Might drop in at your place this week. Wednesday. That OK?'

'Sure,' Sasha would say. Tony would look uncertain that he'd got his message across, and slouch discontentedly back to the bar.

They knew people there that they didn't talk to but cast resentful glares toward, and I wondered what dramas they had spun for themselves or if blood had really been spilled.

When we left the pub the night was colder and the street was black from the rain. People were on the footpath, talking and shivering, making plans for next weekend and kissing in the dark. Sasha walked ahead, his coat flashing at his heels, to where his car was parked on the far side of the road. Andy and I straggled after him, our reflections on the wet bitumen shimmering silver with street light. A stationwagon pulled away from the kerb and headed straight for us and Andy and I froze, poised like rabbits in the middle of the tram tracks. When it was too close we sprang to the right, ridiculously flustered because it was probably a joke, and Sasha, who had seen, gave the car and its occupants a considering stare. 'Arseholes,' Andy snapped, but Sasha Johns said nothing.

Sasha owned a coughing little car that had been, not too long ago, a sporty and rather spiffy little car. His group of friends spent a lot of money keeping their cars mobile, for they were necessary tools of their various trades, but Sasha spent least of all. It was part of his power, to ignore his own rules. I climbed clumsily into the back seat, catching my bootlace on the gear stick. Sasha switched on the heater and let the wipers swish back and forth as we started up the hill. After a few minutes I realised we were following the wagon that had nearly run over Andy and me, and that we were getting closer.

'Louie,' said Sasha, 'there's a carton of milk back there. Can you see it?'

At my feet was a hefty two-litre carton of milk. I passed it to Andy, who shook it and opened it, not just on one side so it had a spout, but on both sides, so it had a gaping square maw. 'Good God,' he spluttered, and pressed himself into his seat. 'Sasha, what the hell . . .'

Peering through the gap between the seats, the stench of it made me woozy. 'There's lumps,' I reported. 'There's more lumps than liquid.'

Sasha chortled merrily. 'It's been sloshing around back there for two weeks,' he said. 'I remembered to buy it, but I kept forgetting to put it in the fridge.'

The smell of it lifted the hair on my arms, gave the alcohol in my system a violent stir. 'It's making me sick,' I muttered.

'You can be sick in a minute. You cannot put your head out the window yet.'

They didn't talk about what they intended to do. It was a thing I would come to notice: none of them needed to explain things to each other. Sasha knew something, had seen something, and Andy trusted him enough to go without being told what it was.

As we drew alongside the vehicle of our enemies Andy spun down his window and hurled the carton out. It was a beautiful, curving, graceful shot; Andy had played cricket as a teenager. The carton sailed the short distance between the cars and plunged through the driver's window. From where I was, perched on my knees on the dusty padding of Sasha's car seat, I saw the milk wash across the inside of the wagon's windscreen, yellow against the patches of fog that the fresh air had not yet blasted from the glass. The carton bounced off the chest of the front-seat passenger and disappeared. 'We should go now,' said Andy: Sasha pressed the accelerator and we zoomed away as the car beside us faltered like a crippled thing, veering blindly to the kerb.

I swung forward and goggled at them. 'My God!' I squealed. 'Andy! Sasha!'

They were giggling to themselves and didn't answer me. The reek of the milk was lingering and I put a hand over my face. 'They'll chase us,' I prophesied through my fingers. 'They know what car we're driving. They'll go to the police.'

A yip of laughter escaped Andy, who put his knuckles to his mouth as if to stuff it back in. I turned to gaze at the hamstrung car. I could see its smeared windscreen even from that distance, the great dripping streaks that marked the carton's flight. 'They'll catch us and kill us,' I whimpered, hunkering down in my seat. 'They'll never get that smell out. Drive faster, Sasha.'

'I thought you said you were sick. You're yapping a lot for a sick person.'

But he did drive faster, and the wagon grew indistinguishable from other lights and shapes, and then a dip in the land took the scraps of the scene away. I felt safer once it was out of sight, and I laughed, and my laughter sounded odd and lonely, coming out so late. Andy and Sasha were no longer even smiling, and might have forgotten or grown bored by what they'd so recently done. Andy was looking out the window and after a minute he asked, 'Where are we going?'

'I do not know,' answered Sasha.

'I don't want,' I said, 'to go home.'

So we went to Sasha's place.

He lived with his parents and his sister in an enormous house in a street full of enormous houses and trees. It was months before I got to look inside the house because Sasha lived in a very self-contained miniature house at the end of the garden. He had a kitchen and a bathroom and a bedroom, and another room, the largest, where he entertained his guests and ran the business. 'Sasha,' Andy would say, 'was driven to crime through the tedium of being rich.' Andy had been fifteen and working part-time at the grill of the local hamburger joint when he first met Sasha and the others, but Sasha had never held a proper job; Andy had gone to university to get the dogs of Social Security off his tail but Sasha hardly knew what a dole form looked like. Life had been startlingly easy for him. 'His mother is a pharmacist,' Andy would explain. 'Sasha inherited his interest in drugs from her.' Sasha's father was an orthodontist, but I never asked what the son had inherited from him.

Sasha's friends would park their cars around the bungalow and over time they had carved a bald trenched turning-circle in the grass. There was a car stopped in the circle and we pulled up behind it. Lights were on in the bungalow and music was thumping the door. Inside, a thin young man was dancing with a golden retriever, and the dog's reluctance had ruckled the rug and knocked a glass from the coffee table. When it saw us, the animal wrenched its paws from its partner's grip and bounded across the room to Sasha, a swirl of golden delight and relief. 'Don't dance with my dog,' said Sasha.

'I've been waiting for hours,' sulked the thin guy, and flopped into a chair. 'She likes dancing. Don't you. Don't you, Jemima.'

Jemima ignored everybody if Sasha was nearby, and she ignored Flynn now. She had her own beanbag and she curled up in it, feathers of hair about her snout, her dewy eyes fixed on her master. Flynn looked, instead, at me. 'Hello,' he said. 'Who are you?'

And I remembered that I was a stranger here, with a long way to go. I told him my name and knew he scarcely heard, hardly listening. At first sight I thought I would hate Flynn, hate the importance of him, hate his baby face, but it is Flynn I think most often of now, when years have passed and I'm as old, now, as he was then; I wonder if he is happy and if he is all right. He was Sasha's best friend and the pair of them worked as a professional team: Sasha heard rumour and Flynn investigated its truth, Sasha proposed plans and Flynn calculated risk. Sasha's bungalow was a place of rendezvous and sanctuary but it was Flynn who always sat where he could see those who approached the door. He supplied equipment the business needed and he never failed to produce the required goods. He occasionally profited more than others because he contributed more than most, but sometimes he would decline to accept what was given him. 'What I do,' he told me solemnly, 'I do for love.'

There was beer in the refrigerator, and a bowl of mull on the coffee table. I sat on the couch and clicked my fingers at the dog, who ignored me. Sasha opened the bottles and Flynn packed the pipe, chatting as he did so about the day he'd had, in which he'd done nothing. No one mentioned the flying carton of milk. Flynn turned ceremonious when he proffered the pipe to me.

'Ladies first.'

I'd never smoked dope before, and I didn't know how to, so I did what I'd seen done on the tele: I put my mouth to the pipe and a flame to the cone and drew a deep breath. The mull glowed wanly and nothing else happened. 'Put your finger over the shotty,' Andy hinted beneath his breath. I glanced at Sasha and Flynn, who were politely looking elsewhere. I put my thumb over the air-hole and tried again.

Later, when it was after three in the morning and swamp creatures, roused by the drugs, were cavorting in my head, Sasha and I sat by the edge of the swimming pool watching Andy do laps back and forth through the freezing water. Flynn had crashed out beside Jemima the retriever, who had risen in a huff and left him on the beanbag, and come to sleep beside us on the decking, under the moon. Her paws scratched the wood as she dreamed.

I'd been talking for hours, it seemed, and I still hadn't run out of things to say. I was convinced that what I was saying was fascinating indeed. There's a drug word for the phenomenon: *babbling*. I was shamelessly babbling, and the fact that Sasha simply sat there, saying little, did nothing to shut me up.

'I remember where I've seen you,' I drawled.

'On the train.'

'Yeah, but I remember *the situation*. I didn't remember the *situation* before, but now I do.'

He scratched at a fleck on his boot. 'What, then.'

'On my way to uni one day . . . it was morning . . . it was warm . . . you were on the train . . .'

. . . I'd been on a train going to classes and I noticed him sitting alone, without bags or books or anything to say where he was going or why. The carriage was almost empty and he was staring blankly out the window; I had my sunglasses on and, so shielded, was free to stare at him. The train slid into a station and a blind man stepped through the carriage doors, waving his white-tipped cane. Sasha watched the man shuffle for a moment, disoriented, arms extended hopefully. He fumbled into metal handrailing, turned doubtfully, stepped on a gob of chewy.

'Here,' said Sasha. He rose from his seat and reached for the man's wrist, guiding him into the place opposite himself.

'Thank you,' said the blind man.

'That's all right,' said Sasha Johns.

It was as much as they said to each other, at least in the time I travelled with them. But Sasha glared like a wolf at people who got on at other stations and they obediently kept away, finding seats where they wouldn't stumble against the blind man or accidentally kick his cane, or distract him with their talk. I had longed to tell Sasha that I thought he'd done a good thing, but I feared I'd get glared at as well.

'Well?' Sasha prompted.

'Well what?'

'What about the train?'

'Oh,' I said, 'I've forgotten.'

Andy, arms crossed over the edge of the pool, laughed. 'Don't give her any more cones,' he said, 'she's lost the plot,' and sank into the water. Sasha, head on his knees, looked silently at me through the darkness. I hadn't forgotten, and neither had he.

'You should go,' he sighed. 'Let me get to bed.'

Andy lived not far away, and I lived not far from him, so the two of us walked, Andy shivering as we went. We reached his gate first and he said, 'Come in.'

I hadn't had sex with anyone before. I was apprehensive, but virginity was becoming an embarrassing weight. I was nearly nineteen and had spent too long being ugly and shy. It was a night for change.

He had a big untidy bed in a small untidy room and we had to be quiet. I didn't tell him I hadn't done it before. I was nearly nineteen, after all. I took my clothes off and tried not to look at him, and hoped he wouldn't look too closely at me. In bed we kissed and tickled and I giggled stupidly, wondering if I was enjoying this. I felt him pressing bluntly against me, an alien sensation down there that almost made me laugh, it was so bizarre, and then all of a sudden I'd lost it, glad to be rid of it, welcomed the slight, peculiar pain. I held tight to him thinking that what Sasha said was true, I'd never forget Andy, he had claimed a place in my life and I'd look on him with fondness forever, I'd never hate him, no matter what happened. He asked me to stay but I said no, I had to go home, I had an essay to write the next day. He would have walked with me but I wanted to go alone. It was almost morning and soon it would be light. So I walked home alone, new.

So now we're all of us in trouble. Alexandra says she'll tell the story if we'll try to look at it from her point of view, and not interrupt while she's thinking. We're sitting in the loft and her stuff is all around us, lumps of clay and wooden tools and heaps of other junk, and there's a funny smell in the air, a smell like earth gone bad, or poisoned. Alex says it's just the smell of clay.

The whole time she speaks she hardly looks at us – she looks at the floor and out the window now and then, as if to check that everything is still out there, and that she is still here. But she hardly looks at us. I only look at her sometimes; mostly I look at the floor. I smoke sixteen cigarettes while she's talking, and the smoke makes for the window like a ghost leaving the room. Mostly we say nothing, just listening to her.

Usually I hate spending time getting out of trouble, but here in the loft I don't mind.

She met him at the pub she sometimes went to when Kate was on the afternoon shift and the pottery shop was busy enough to keep Alexandra back till five or six. Both of them would change their clothes – Alex out of her smudgy artist's smock, Kate out of her greasy chef's coat – and they'd meet at the Rainbow and have a few drinks before going out for dinner, or skipping dinner altogether if they both felt like it. The Rainbow is one of those tiny pubs on a corner that have been done up just enough to be comfortable, and its owners know what the patrons do and don't like. They like bands that aren't too hard on the ear, something like Irish, and they don't like pinball machines or poker machines or any signage for American alcohols. It's not a rough crowd, there's never any fights: it's a pub where arty people go, and musicians, and people who think they are musicians and make annoying comments to the band at the end of each song. Single mothers go there, and sometimes there's a kid running round with dreadlocks in its hair. Everyone's friendly; everyone's wearing vests and, if it's cold, everyone's wearing long black shabby coats that the fire in the corner and the press of the crowd will eventually make them want to take off – but they can't, because there's never enough tables and chairs and there is nowhere to drape it unless over your arm. Near the fire will be an old drunk who'll be harmless, who'll try to make conversation with anyone that strays near him to say that twenty, thirty years ago he knew this pub in its heyday, when it was full of criminals. There will always be some tall skinny guy who'll get talking to this drunk, and soon wish he hadn't, and try to inch away. It is a nice pub; the crowd is interesting to watch; it is the sort of place where strangers talk to each other in the toilets and the band doesn't care if someone accidentally falls amongst the drums. Which happens, pretty frequently.

Alex and Kate arrive early enough to get two of the stools around the big horseshoe bar, and because Alex didn't stop for lunch the peanuts Kate buys are the first thing she's eaten all day, and the beers make her feel woozy after two or three. By eight o'clock the place is starting to fill up and the band has arrived and is unpacking their gear in the tiny space that's allotted them. There's still one or two empty tables because people sometimes prefer to stand, so it's good, not too crowded, not so empty that everyone notices each other. It's just after eight and Alex is starting to feel the effects of no food. Kate is saying, 'Every single person who came into the restaurant today was an arsehole. *Every single one.*'

Alex turns to look at her and her head swings, for a moment, out of control. It feels like it might break from her neck and roll across the floor. She clamps her hands around her throat and asks in alarm, 'Did my head just lurch?'

Kate looks at her. 'What?'

'My head – did it just bounce weirdly from one side to the other?'

Kate frowns. 'What?'

'Like a pendulum – like a cannonball – like this – '

Alexandra lets her head wonk and Kate narrows her eyes, as if there is something distasteful going on. Alexandra ignores the look and checks her neck and shoulders carefully. 'It seems all right,' she says uncertainly. 'I think it's fixed now.'

Kate nods for the bargirl to get them two more, and something else for Alex to eat.

They're starting to be jostled occasionally: it's only a tiny pub and everyone wants to be in it. A lot of the bar space is taken up by cappuccino machines and irritating ornaments and the thick pillars that hold the building together. So Alex and Kate are sitting in one of the few good spaces where it's possible to catch the attention of the girl behind the bar and people are coming close to them all the time. When Kate goes to the toilet Alex has to guard her space forcefully.

Looking back, Alexandra can blame everything on a dollar, a single shining dollar coin that was dropped at the foot of her stool. She didn't need it, but she stepped off the chair and picked it up. 'Look,' she says. 'Look what I found.'

'That guy dropped it,' says Kate.

Alex looks around. 'What guy?'

Kate nods. 'That guy sitting by himself.'

'That guy,' says Alex. 'I know that guy. I've seen him before.'

'He's a babe,' says Kate. 'That guy is a babe.'

Alex stares at the guy, turning the coin in her palm. 'I'm going to talk to that guy,' she decides. 'Are you coming with me?'

'Do you want me to?'

Alex thinks. 'No, you stay here and mind the seats. Then I'll have somewhere to run if he's awful.'

She walks over to the guy's table and says, 'Hello.'

He's sitting alone, hogging a whole table to himself, his single beer sitting in front of him and the rest of the table just vacant, wasted space. He looks up at her and she thinks, My God, he's a god. He's the best-looking guy she's ever seen. She can only conclude he's waiting for his girlfriend.

'You dropped this,' she says, and places the dollar on the table, in the centre of the laminated emptiness.

'Oh,' he says. 'Thank you.'

'I've seen you before,' Alex says. 'You walk past the shop where I work. And then you walk back again.'

'With my lunch,' he says.

'A bread roll and a chocolate milk.'

He smiles. 'I didn't know I was being watched.'

'Oh, you're not,' she says immediately. 'I just see you. I don't watch you.'

'Where do you work?'

'In the pottery shop.' She's got a good job, though she only does it part-time. She sits at a wheel and spins clay, and if you go into the shop or even shade your eyes against the window you can see her sitting there, see her making something nice out of a dirty lump of clay, right before your eyes.

'Oh, yeah,' he says. 'I know that shop. I've never been inside.'

'No,' she acknowledges, and wishes she hadn't said that. She looks down at the coin and when he doesn't say anything she says, 'Well, I better go.'

'I'm not waiting for anyone,' he tells her. She recognises this as an invitation and her heart thumps in her chest.

'I've left my friend alone . . .' she says, worried by this difficulty, and she has a disloyal moment of wishing Kate was somewhere far, far away.

'Bring her over,' says the god. 'You're getting a bit squashed at the bar, anyway.'

So Alex calls Kate over, and tells her to bring their drinks. They sit down in the chairs that come with his table. Kate lets Alex sit closest to the guy, and Alex repents her disloyal moment. Kate knows the rules, she won't trespass on what Alexandra has staked out as her own.

They tell each other their names and then it seems there's nothing much to say: the guy looks at them as if conversation is their responsibility alone. Alex fumbles for a topic, and Kate watches the guy and it strikes her as rude, his silence. Even a bit cruel. But she's prepared to consider that maybe he is just shy.

Alexandra casts her eyes around the pub and finally back to her new friend. 'Do you always eat your lunch alone?' she asks. 'Just you and your bread roll?'

'Yes,' he says. 'Just me and the Vegemite.'

'Always the same, every day?'

'I don't like too much variety.'

Alexandra laughs, though it wasn't funny. 'Kate's a chef,' she says.

'That's nice,' he replies.

Kate comes to her friend's rescue. 'So, Daniel,' she says. 'What are you doing here, all by yourself?'

'Why not?' he shoots back. 'I like this band.'

'Oh,' Kate says. She adds, 'Yeah, they're very good.'

'I think it's ridiculous,' says Daniel, 'this idea that, everywhere you go, you have to be there with someone, or else you can't be enjoying yourself. I like to have a drink by myself sometimes, that's all.'

Kate, annoyed by his tone, says, 'Maybe we should leave, then.'

'It's up to you. But I'd like it if you stayed.'

Kate looks at him warily. She doesn't like him. After a couple of sentences she's smelling something bad. She decides then and there that she'll do nothing more to help this conversation along.

Not Alexandra, though: she's not by nature a harsh judge and she forgives people their quirks. That, and the fact that every time she looks at the guy she is gobsmacked by his beauty. He's got black hair and blue eyes and if he's a little thin around the lips, well, no one's perfect, but Daniel is close.

The band has started tuning up and the sound they make is

broken and unpleasant, jarring its way through the voices of the crowd. Alexandra looks down at the coin, circular on the square table; on the table are beer mats and beer glasses, and the coin glows golden in these dull surrounds like a portal into a better place. Like a lost, immaculate droplet of time.

'I was on a tram, once,' she says. 'It was years ago, I was only a kid, only thirteen or fourteen. It was back when the old trams were running, before they scrapped them, the old rattling trams with seats along the walls and an open area in the middle that everyone sat facing into. It was about lunchtime and there were hardly any people on the tram so we all had a seat and we all sat a fair distance from each other, like you do when there's enough space. And lying in the centre of the floor of this tram was a dollar. It was the year they started making dollar coins, the time when paper dollars were still around and you'd see the coins but they were pretty rare. So there it was, this shining gold dollar, pristine, spangling, something we'd hardly ever seen, lying in the centre of this empty space and all of us tram travellers staring, staring, staring at it, transfixed. We could hardly breathe. It was dazzling, this coin, it was entrancing, none of us could tear our eyes off it. It jiggled to the movement of the tram, it was dancing, rapping the floorboards. Every one of us, we wanted it. We hungered for it. We drooled. I think that if anyone had moved a muscle towards it, the rest of us would have pounced on that person and beaten him to death. We told ourselves,

It's only a stupid dollar, but we didn't believe it, we wanted it, and no one dared move. It was agony. We tried to ignore it, we tried as hard as we could, but it was too beautiful . . .'

She stops, struck by the feeling that this is a really boring story and that she's making a fool of herself. She glances at Kate, who has actually turned around to watch the band. Alex grips her glass with both her hands and takes a gulp from it. If she drinks it fast she'll have an excuse to go to the bar and from there they can get away from here.

'Go on,' says Daniel suddenly. 'What happened to the dancing coin?'

She lifts her face to him, forgiving everything at the sound of those sweet words: at that instant she knows what will happen, how the rest of this night will turn out. 'The tram stopped and a man got on. The first thing he saw was the dollar. He stopped, bent over, picked it up and put it in his pocket. That was the last we saw of it. The rest of us, we died a little at that moment.'

Daniel smiles at her; Alex knows Kate has returned her attention to them and that she's seen this particular smile.

Daniel uses a fingertip to push his dollar toward her. 'Here,' he says, 'you can take this coin instead.'

Alexandra blushes with pleasure at this flash of charm but says, 'No, it's all right, I've gotten over the thing.'

'Take it,' he insists. 'It feels like it's lucky.'

So she takes it, puts it in her pocket.

Seeing Andy would spark a joy in me that no one has ever matched since, but not because I adored him. I didn't adore him; I liked him, he was funny, and he was fun to be near. I liked lying around with him, I liked meeting him between classes for the pauper's lunch that was all we could afford, and I liked it that he rang me and that everyone knew he was taken, taken by *me*, but I didn't love *him*. I loved the paraphernalia that came with him. It started to seem that, before Andy, I hadn't known anything about anything: I had never learned a single detail of life. Andy changed everything, and I gathered new knowledge like a creature hoarding food, greedily, things I could graze over in private, that I could sit back and examine proudly, that might sustain me should times become lean. I learned how to pull a pipe without choking and I learned that boys wake with stiffies that have to be teased down with a pee. I learned to see the invisible lines on a billiard table and I learned how to connect a Nintendo to the TV. Flynn taught me to play poker and let me win until he thought I'd won enough. Sasha lent me books and I read Kerouac and Hunter Thompson, and he let me keep his Lou Reed

CD because I liked it so much. Andy hired classic films and he and I watched them from the comfort of his double bed. I'd been to the university's doctor and got a prescription for the Pill and the sight of those little pink and white tablets made me feel grand and forthright, I stopped being embarrassed when I took off my clothes. I wagged a lot of classes to hang around with him but when I went to school I volunteered answers more often, less afraid of appearing half-witted, and my marks went up after it dawned on me where I was going wrong in my approach to critical analysis. I dyed my hair a bloody red and my mother shrieked to see me, but I thought it looked good. I flipped the calendar and Andy and I had been going out for a month, for six weeks, for seven. Life at home began to seem intolerably tedious and when I was there I would fret about what I might be missing. My parents invited Andy to dinner and he came dressed in some of Sasha's clothes, big on him but better than his own. My parents complained less, then, about me spending nights at a boy's house. They didn't believe me when I told them I always slept on the couch, but they pretended they did. When my mother asked me about the new friends I was seeing so often, I lied and said I'd met them at university, and when I described them I dipped them in silver plating and polished them up clean for her.

Winter stripped the last leaves from the trees, soaked the earth to slush and stopped the grass from growing. As I got to know his friends better I would badger Andy to take me to Sasha's place, where something was always happening. One day a trailbike turned up at the bungalow and Andy gave me a dink through the suburb's streets;

I was jerked from the saddle and into the mud when I tried to ride it alone around Sasha's garden. Flynn gave me a bottle of mescal for my nineteenth birthday and at his encouragement I closed my eyes and chewed up the worm, gagging at the thought through my hangover the next day.

My old friend Cassy invited me to her family's beach house when the semester holidays started, but I said I couldn't go. 'Why not?' she asked.

'I'm going away,' I said, 'with Andy.'

'All you ever do is hang around with Andy,' she said, petulantly.

'I do not. I went to the beach house last year, and the year before, and the year before that. This year I'm going to the mountains.'

'With Andy.'

I looked at her darkly. 'So?'

'So, you hardly ever hang around with me any more.'

'We've got different lives now, Cass,' I told her. 'I've got new friends, you've got new friends – '

'I haven't got any new friends,' she corrected. 'You were happy enough to have me as a friend when we were at school.'

'I'm still your *friend*,' I sighed. 'Cass, stop behaving like a child.'

She took no notice of that, I could see. 'When are you going to introduce me to these friends of yours, anyway?' she asked. 'When do I get to meet Andy?'

I looked at her, grappling for the words. She wore a baby-pink cardigan and she had clips clawing back her straight, mousy hair. She had been a target of much ridicule at school and even though I knew her well, knew how barbed her humour could be and how kind and decent she always was, even I sometimes sniggered at her. I pictured her standing in the middle of the bungalow with her smudgy blue eyeliner and the patches of rouge on her round white cheeks, and everyone looking from her to me and back again. They would laugh at her, and she was my friend, she was my past and all the details I'd glossed over in talking to them about it, so they would laugh at me too. I clenched my teeth and swore it would not happen.

'I'll introduce you to them one day,' I said. 'Look – I'm only going away with Andy for a weekend. I'll come down to the beach after that.'

And I did, and stayed for five cold days of walking the shoreline and playing Monopoly, and when I got home I found that I had missed an afternoon at the pub when Flynn, dizzy with the combined effects of a dentist's needle and alcohol, had regaled his table with a stream of nonsense that made people cackle with laughter, and that Sasha had got a new video game and everyone knew how to play it except me. I made a stern promise to myself: it would never happen again, no matter how Cassy begged.

I learned the history of their friendship from Flynn, who would always talk to me if he thought I was being forgotten. Flynn had known Hastings since they were kids because Flynn had shifted into a house near to Hastings's and little boys seek each other out, following the sound of bike tyres on driveways and the scent of skinned knees. Hastings went to the same expensive secondary school as Sasha, and thus Sasha had been introduced to Flynn. Flynn had met

Andy when they worked together at the hamburger place, captaining the grill in the kitchen and dealing drugs in the shrubbery down the back of the carpark.

'Everyone knew,' Flynn reminisced. 'Everyone except the manager and the happy families knew exactly what was going on. People would come in and wave to us behind the counter and then Andy or I would say we had to take a slash and we'd go out and sell some hooch, and the guy would smoke it in the laneway and come back inside for munchies. We must have had fifty or sixty people who used to buy from us there. It was a good job.'

'Didn't you ever get caught? No one ever dobbed you in?'

Flynn shook his head. 'No way. We were far too convenient. The place was almost always open.'

Flynn liked to tell his stories, and Andy would elaborate upon them, but I would never have discovered the details of the business if it hadn't been for the Handbrake. Flynn and Andy would not have told me about that if they could have left me, instead, in ignorance.

We went to Sasha's place late one stormy afternoon and opened the door to a gale. The Handbrake was whirling around the room in the full grip of her perpetual fury. Flynn was backed against a wall and he had the hunted look of all men faced with a woman they loathe and dread. He saw us in the doorway, salvation, and almost fell to his knees. The Handbrake spun and stared at Andy. 'You!' she bawled. 'Where's David?'

I knew of her, for she was legend, but I'd never met her and suddenly, terribly, didn't want to. 'Hastings isn't with us,' said Andy, bravery in his voice.

'I *told* you, Elly, he's with Sasha.'

'Bloody Sasha,' she spat. 'Where's he? Or don't you know *that*, either?'

'Elsbeth, this is Louie,' Andy interrupted, and Elsbeth wheeled to me.

'Get rid of him,' she ordered me curtly. 'Piss him off. If you want to do something good for yourself, piss him off.'

'Elly – '

'I mean it!' she barked. 'You're a pack of arseholes and you know you are! I'm sick of the lot of you! David isn't hanging around here any more. You can find yourselves some other idiot to kick heads for you.'

Flynn giggled, unwisely. She approached him with quick biting steps. He wasn't tall, Flynn, and they met eye to eye. He was fragile, and so was she, but she looked capable, at that moment, of tearing him into pieces with her manicured and bejewelled hands. 'I know everything about you,' she informed him ominously, as he swallowed his mirth. They were frightened of her; everyone was frightened of her. Hastings was terrified of her. Together, the pair of them were like some huge placid bear being led from the nose by some very aggressive, very neurotic, impeccably groomed chihuahua. 'I know *everything* about you,' the Handbrake said to Flynn, jabbing him in the throat with a scarlet fingernail, 'and I wouldn't be laughing, if I were you.'

'I'm not – '

'No. Not now.'

Elsbeth swung away from him, kicking the rug from the floor. Her face was hard and pretty and she fixed her furious eyes on me. 'It will happen to you too, you know,' she warned. 'Whenever you want him around, he'll be here with this bunch of – *bastards* – useless. They're useless. They're a bunch of useless criminal drug-addict shit-head *bastards*.'

'Elly – '

She ignored Flynn. 'We were meant to be going to the beach this morning,' she told me. 'Hastings and me. I like the beach in winter, I like it, I don't care if it's raining, I never care about stuff like that. I *adapt*, I make room in my life for everything. But David had to come here first, to see his darling Sasha, that *shit* – just ten minutes, he said, just to pick up something. I knew it was a lie but I let him go, to see if once, just *once*, he would keep his word. And here I am, still waiting for him to come home so we can go to the beach and have one day in peace. One day isn't very much, it's not asking for much. Is it. I never get to go anywhere. It's been ages since we went anywhere . . . I made a picnic and everything. I made a cake.'

The room went silent, and Elsbeth's gaze travelled to the bowl of mull on the table. 'Do you know what they do?' she asked me, not caring if I did or not. 'They rob people.'

'Elly – ' Flynn chirped.

'They sell drugs. Not just dope. Anything you want.'

'Elsbeth – '

'They steal.'

'Handbrake!' Flynn yelped, fatally. It caught her attention all right. She strode up to him and slapped him powerfully across the face. His head smacked the wall and he staggered sideways.

'Don't you call me that!' she screamed. 'You miserable cretin! You shit-for-brains!'

Flynn cowered, there was no denying it. Elsbeth reeled to face me.

'They bash people up and they hassle them for money and they steal anything they can get their hands on and they act like pricks every day of their lives!' she roared. 'They don't care about anyone! *He* doesn't care about *you*! Take my advice and split and kick his poxy little brain out as you go!'

And then, almost sneaking past her wrath, the sound of a car easing to a standstill outside. Elsbeth pricked her ears, yanked the door open and flew out like an enraged canary.

'Holy shit,' muttered Flynn, touching his jaw tenderly.

'Let's go,' said Andy. 'I don't want to be around to see this.'

So we exited on tiptoe out the back of the bungalow and skirted the building, keeping low to the ground, stifling laughter at the sound of Hastings being skinned alive. 'What about Sasha?' I asked, knowing he was snagged somewhere in the massacre, and Flynn replied, 'Nothing can save him now.'

We went to the pub, and stayed there through the storm.

There was hardly anyone at the hotel but I hunched against the table and kept my voice low. 'Tell me,' I said.

'There's nothing to tell.'

'She wouldn't say those things about *nothing*.'

'We're without sin,' sniffed Flynn, his chin haughtily high. 'The Handbrake is a compulsive liar.'

'Why do you call her Handbrake?'

'She doesn't let Hastings go.'

'That's not how she sees it.'

'It's *true*, though,' gasped Flynn. 'Hastings is thoroughly henpecked and tyrannised. You saw her, Louie, she's a beast. She's a harridan psycho ball-breaking bitch. She's got three sixes on her forehead.'

'Come on, I just want to know – '

'I just want this, I just want that – '

'Your face is still really red, Flynn. That slap must have hurt like hell. You don't want another one, do you? Tell me.'

Flynn slid his elbows across the table until his green gaze was level with mine. 'It's not that we don't *want* to tell you, Louie,' he whispered, 'it's that you don't want to *know*. If we told you, we'd have to *kill* you.'

I sat up straight. 'Tell me,' I begged. 'I want to know. It's not fair. I deserve to know. You're being my friends but you've got this whole life that you're not telling. I only want to be told – '

'Lou,' Andy sighed, swilling the dregs of his beer, 'Elsbeth was right. We're idiots.'

I swung my head to look at him, my fists closed tight. 'Don't you think you can trust me?'

'It's not that,' Andy said, but he didn't say what it was. I knew, though: they didn't want to share. They didn't want to share their secrets with someone who had done nothing to deserve the hearing, someone they hardly knew, someone who might not be loyal forever and could one day have reason to bear a grudge. I subsided into silence, and after some spiky minutes of me staring moodily at the wall and them seeking pathetically for a distracting topic, I tucked the subject up my sleeve and found them another. There was time, I could wait. Not very long, and in the end I didn't have to.

We left the Greyhound at ten that night, hazy with watery beer and the seven packets of corn chips we'd eaten for dinner. On our way through the empty Club Room, Flynn noted that the bar was unattended and so ducked behind it and lifted a bottle of tequila from where it stood. 'Flynn?' I inquired, as he pressed the bottle to my chest, and he whispered, 'That's a present. For being denied.'

'I don't want it – '

'It's almost full,' he said, hurt. 'It's even got a jigger.'

'Hide it,' Andy advised.

I slipped the bottle amongst the folds of my coat and we hurried out to the carpark, the gravel crunching under our boots. It had stopped raining but the sky was flashy with faraway lightning. We climbed into Andy's car and drove off. 'She says she's our friend, but you notice she doesn't offer us a drink,' said Flynn.

I pulled the jigger from the bottle and passed the tequila to him.

Andy had switched the heater on and the hot breeze hissing through the air vents was making me feel murky and drunk. I watched the jigger rocking on my thighs. It was an interesting thing, smooth and silver and surgical. The way it rocked made me queasy, so I took my eyes off it. I slumped down, pressed my hands into the car seat and let the springs bounce them up to me. I wondered why I always got the back seat. 'Hey,' I said. 'Hey, you guys. How come I always get the back seat?'

'See it?' Flynn asked.

'Yeah,' said Andy.

'See what?'

'We'll be stopped.'

Andy nodded slowly. His eyes went to the mirror and I looked out the rear window to see what he saw. A police car was cruising behind us, and getting closer.

'Lou.'

'What?' I stuttered, eyes like saucers. I suddenly felt very sober. I also felt a strong inclination to be elsewhere. 'What, Flynn?'

'Say nothing to them. Believe nothing they say. OK?'

'. . . OK.'

The police car switched on its lights and blueness swept over my hands.

'Nothing. Louie?'

'OK,' I breathed.

Andy pulled into the kerb. The police car drew up behind us. Two men in uniform climbed out and walked to our windows. I had never been that close to policemen before. Their clothes fit snugly as a second skin. 'Step out of the vehicle please,' the first of them said.

'All of us?'

'All of you.'

We got out of the car. Flynn skirted the bonnet and I saw, with unspeakable horror, that he was still holding the tequila bottle. He seemed not to notice that he had it and propped it casually on the car, but he didn't let it go.

One policeman was older; he had a thick neat moustache and a firm swollen gut. The other was younger and angular and less fearsome in every aspect. 'Where have you been tonight?' the older cop asked.

'To the Skinny Dog.'

'Been there for long?'

'Since about six this evening.'

'We saw your vehicle in the carpark.'

'. . . Well.'

The cop produced a breathalyser. 'Would you blow into this, please, sir.'

Andy did as he was told. I glanced desperately at Flynn. He wasn't looking at me, and he wasn't looking at the tequila, but he was surreptitiously scratching a sticker from the label of the bottle. I knew what that sticker said: it said GREYHOUND HOTEL, $29.95.

The cops peered intently at the tester for a moment before the older one tucked the gadget away. 'Can we go now?' asked Andy.

'Nope.' The fat cop turned, and gazed at Flynn and me. 'Where'd you get the tequila?' he asked.

'We bought it at the Vicky Greene,' Flynn replied.

'Your mate said you were at the Greyhound.'

'We were. But we walked up to the Victoria to meet someone. The Skinny and the Vicky are walking distance from each other, as you know. Or do you only drive?'

I nearly gagged, but the cop didn't twitch. 'You're a smartarse, aren't you.'

'It's in my nature,' Flynn confirmed breezily.

'Yeah, it is. A smartarse.'

Flynn smirked but the cop didn't see. He had opened the door of Andy's car and stuck his head inside. Flynn's thumbnail attacked the price sticker with a frenzy. I shuffled my feet and hugged my coat closer to me; it was cold, and the gruesomeness of our situation made it seem colder, and my jaw started juddering. Andy was looking at me and I smiled at him weakly but the thinner cop was watching him and Andy's face stayed expressionless.

'What's this?'

The cop brought out the jigger and waved it under Flynn's nose.

'That? That looks to me like a spirit pourer.'

'You're really funny, aren't you?' the cop flared. 'You're a really, really funny guy.'

Flynn thought about this. 'Well, I'm not funny all the time,' he admitted.

'Shut your head, or I'll shut it for you. Where'd you get the pourer from?'

'It's mine,' said Andy. The cop turned to him and I saw Flynn succeed, with a final determined gouge, in prising the sticker from the bottle.

'It's kind of mine, in a way,' Andy rambled. 'I bought the car from a friend and there was all sorts of shit in it. Stuff in it. Clothes and tools and stuff. That was in it.'

The fat cop laughed. 'Lots of *friends* in your life, aren't there? You must be popular people. Friends at the pub, friends selling cars. Friends who aren't here to contradict your story.'

Andy shrugged lamely. The cop looked back at Flynn and me, shrouded in the whiteness of police-vehicle headlights. 'You know what I think?'

'No idea. What?'

'I think you're bullshitting. I reckon you nicked this from a pub around here, and we're going to find out if you did. You – ' he pointed to Andy, 'follow us. You, funny boy, get into the police vehicle.'

'What for?' Flynn squawked. 'Where are we going? Am I being arrested? What's the charge?'

The fat cop leaned very close to him, said, 'I'm starting to lose patience with you.' Flynn clamped his mouth shut. The thin cop opened the door of the police car and Flynn climbed into the rear seat; the door was slammed after him and he sat in the gloom, looking furious.

'Where are we going?' Andy asked.

'Just follow us, sir.'

So Andy and I got back in our car and followed the police down the long wet road that led straight to the Victoria Greene Hotel. I was feeling very sick. I felt sicker when Andy murmured, 'We're in deep shit here.'

And when we reached the Vicky Greene, all the lights were off and it was locked up tight. Andy laughed aloud and flexed his fingers against the steering-wheel. 'Is this good?' I asked. 'That it's closed?'

'They were going to ask if we'd bought the tequila at the bottle shop. But the bottle shop is – '

'Is closed.' I marvelled at the fact.

'They'll have to let us go now, they can't prove anything.'

We looked expectantly at the police vehicle, watching for Flynn to emerge. The blue-and-white car sat squatly beside the kerb, its hazard lights blinking, pondering its next move. The fat cop's arm appeared, adjusted the side mirror minutely.

Then, the cop's arm waved us forward. 'You bastard,' Andy breathed.

'What?' I wailed. 'Where now?'

'The Greyhound. It's only walking distance, after all.'

'But that's worse! That's worse, isn't it?'

'Be cool,' he said firmly. He looked at me and smiled reassuringly. 'They'll leave you alone,' he promised. 'They don't hassle girls.'

At the Greyhound, the scene of the crime, Flynn was ordered

out of the police vehicle. Then the older cop marched up to my door.

'Will you come with me, Miss.'

'Me?' I gaped. 'Why me?'

'Just come along, please.'

I didn't have time to look at Andy, or to ask him anything. I climbed from the car and stumbled after the policeman and Flynn, into the hotel. I'm going to cry, I remember thinking: I am definitely going to bawl.

There was a handful of people in the public bar. All of them stared at us and their conversation dipped as it always does in the presence of the law, as if everyone is guilty of something forbidden. The cop beckoned the bartender to us, brandished the tequila and asked, 'Do you sell this product in your bottle shop?'

'Sure,' said the bartender.

'Everyone – '

'Shut up!' the cop shouted at Flynn, and then he looked at me.

For a moment I thought I'd say nothing, that I'd been struck miraculously dumb, and then I heard myself say, 'Everyone sells that brand of tequila.'

'That's true,' agreed the bartender.

The cop kept his eyes fixed on mine. 'Your mates say this was bought at the Victoria Greene Hotel. Were you with them when they acquired it?'

'Of course – '

The cop wheeled like a rhino to Flynn. Only the presence of the bartender and the eavesdropping public saved Flynn's thin skin at that moment. But maybe I did too, a bit, by squeaking, 'Yes, I did. I went with them.'

The cop turned stiffly. In the light I could see the gun holstered at his hip. It looked heavy and its butt was worn. He'd probably shot quite a few people with it. 'Then you would know how much it cost,' he said. 'Wouldn't you, Miss.'

'It cost about thirty dollars,' I replied. 'Twenty-nine or thirty dollars. Something like that.'

The cop glanced at the bartender, who nodded.

'Can we go now please?' pestered Flynn. 'Now you've had your fun?'

'Shut it.'

We were shepherded out the door and over the road again. 'In the police vehicle,' ordered the cop. 'Both of you.'

I glanced toward Andy's car but couldn't see him inside it, his windscreen was all reflections. The cop put a hand on top of my head and pressed me into the seat. I'd never been in a police vehicle before. This one was clean and new, and it had that comfortable, new-car smell. We might have been its very first passengers. The heater was on but I was freezing and my teeth knocked together. I was hideously afraid. Flynn leaned over and tapped my arm. When I looked at him he smiled, exuding coolness.

They took us to the police station. I couldn't believe I had been taken to a police station. I had expected to live my whole life without that happening. The walls of the room they put me in were painted cream and there were fluorescent lights on the ceiling. There was a table with a fake wood surface and more vinyl chairs than were needed. I was shut inside it with the thin cop and Flynn was taken somewhere else. Flynn got the fatter, meaner cop.

'Well,' said the thin cop. His voice echoed; it was not a room that kept what was said, its walls were deaf. I shot a glance at him, trying not to look surly or furtive or bold. I knew I should try to look innocent. I thought, I've been innocent all my life, I must remember the look of the thing. I widened my eyes, lifted the corners of my mouth, and looked insane.

'Do you want anything? Coffee? A cigarette?'

'No thanks.'

'What's your name?'

'Louie.'

'Louise. Have you ever been in a place like this before?'

I shook my head. 'It's scary,' I said. The policeman gave a blustery laugh.

'Yes, I suppose it is. But we just want to ask you a few questions.'

'It's scary,' I repeated doggedly.

'Sure you don't want a coffee?'

I did, but coffee would only keep me here longer. I shook my head again and the policeman said nothing. Then he bent forward in his chair. 'Look,' he began, 'Louise. What are you doing hanging around with guys like them? They're losers. We see their type every day. They end up in the courts and in prisons . . . You look like an intelligent person, Louise. What do you do with yourself?'

'I'm a student. At university.'

'You've got an education. You can do better. You know it.'

I pouted, not looking up from the table.

'Do your parents know where you are tonight?'

'. . . I doubt they know I'm at a police station.'

'No, I bet they don't. I can imagine what they'd have to say about it.'

I smiled bleakly, and he seemed pleased. He said, 'Your mate out there with the Senior Constable – he's got a record. Possession. A drunk-and-disorderly. Damage to property. We've linked him to others who are just as bad. Him and his breed, they don't care a great deal about other people.'

I remembered Elsbeth and what she would say to that. 'They're nice to me,' I said. 'They're my friends.'

'Yeah? How long have you known them?'

'A few months.' It sounded feeble when I said it and the cop knew it.

'So they're not your friends, really. They're strangers to you. And that's how it will stay, you know. They're no one's friends. They are interested in themselves and that's all. They'll drop you the minute they decide to. You might not even know why. Not know what you did wrong. Just find yourself alone. An enemy.'

I squirmed in my chair, blew air through my teeth.

'They'll never trouble themselves to save *your* skin, Louise,' he said.

I spluttered, 'It was just a dumb bottle of tequila – '

'It might be theft, Louise. That's a crime.' He gave me a moment to think about this and then said, 'So. Have you ever seen them do anything you'd consider to be against the law?'

'. . . No.'

'Are you sure?'

I glanced at him. 'They're my *friends*,' I repeated hotly. 'I don't think you *understand*.'

He understood then, understood that I had never been on his side, that I was nasty and desperate and possibly a slattern; understood that I was lost and wanted it that way. He sighed tiredly, tapped his fingers on the table. He was young and he wore a shiny wedding ring: somebody was waiting for him somewhere, praying he returned in one piece.

'Please don't bring my mum and dad here,' I said, but I'd lost him also, and he gave me just a tight smile. Then he stood and left the room. I sat bolt upright, crawling with panic, but when minutes went by and nothing else happened I sank in my seat and looked around. There was a window above my head letting in draughts of cold air. It was a high window, pinched as an angry mouth, wired over with mesh. No one could escape through that. A few more minutes went by and I began to wonder what was happening, and to dread it. Then the door swung open and the fat cop walked in.

'Louise,' he said sharply, 'your friend has told us everything. He's told us what happened tonight. You might as well admit it and we can get this thing over with.'

I stared at him, felt tears rise perilously. 'What?'

'*Your . . . friend . . . has . . . admitted*. He has told us what you've been up to tonight. You've been a very bad girl, haven't you? There, have I said it clearly enough for you? Speak English? Comprehend?'

1I couldn't believe it. I looked wildly around the walls. I wanted to scream, to thrash about hysterically on the greasy lino floor. Flynn had told me to say nothing, to believe nothing, but he'd admitted, thrown me in it, what the cop said was true, they weren't the type of people who cared about anyone else –

And Flynn had told me *not to believe anything they said*.

I looked up at the policeman. I gritted my teeth, I wouldn't cry. 'I don't know what Flynn has admitted to,' I stated carefully. 'Whatever he said, he's wrong. We told you what happened. We bought that tequila from the Vicky Greene.'

'From where?' the cop rapped loudly, shouting in my face.

'From the *Vicky Greene*.'

'I can't hear you! From where?'

'From the Vicky Greene!' I yelled.

He glared at me. 'You're making it difficult for yourself,' he said. 'Not for me – for yourself. I'll keep you here all night, if that's what it takes to get the truth out of you.'

'We *told* you the truth.'

'Your mate's *admitted*, young lady. He's got a record already. It's no skin off his nose to see you get one too. You can forget thinking about loyalty.'

A tear skidded down my cheek and I swiped it away. I'd kill Flynn.

I'd get a cricket bat and beat him to death with it. I couldn't believe it. And Flynn had told me not to believe it.

Tears kept falling down my face and I mopped them up with my sleeve. 'Whatever he said to you,' I snivelled, 'he's wrong. I've told you everything.'

'You've told us everything, have you.'

'Yes!' I howled. 'Yes! Let me go!'

'And what you've told us is the truth, according to you.'

'Yes! I want to go home! Let me go home!'

I put my palms to my face and sobbed. That was all I could do now, cry. I could feel the cop watching me with cold flinty cop eyes and I cried and cried shamelessly. I didn't care, I was in for the long haul, I was prepared to bawl all night if it stopped them talking to me. My hands grew wet and snotty and I simply wept. Then I heard the fat cop say, 'Will you please step into the hall.'

In the hall I felt immediately better and stopped crying. Flynn joined us a minute later, escorted by the thin cop. He looked at me, at my streaked blotchy face and wet, bulging eyes, and he looked embarrassed and switched his sights. We were led out the door and bundled into a car. It was raining again. No one said anything as we drove along, and I stared and stared through the window as if I'd never seen the streets before. We arrived at another police station and were directed inside. A policewoman behind the counter said, 'You have to tell us if you were treated well by these officers.'

'Yes,' I answered instantly, 'we were.'

'That one threatened to hit me,' piped Flynn, waving a finger toward the fat cop. The police people ignored him. We signed a couple of papers. Then we were driven back to the place of our incarceration, given our bottle of tequila and the jigger and told we could leave. Flynn walked, but I wanted to run.

Andy was waiting for us, listening to the radio with his eyes closed and a blanket hung around his shoulders. He'd been waiting for almost two hours.

Free, the feeling was exhilarating. Flynn made no mention of my red crying eyes so I was able to gloss over the fact that I had bawled like a baby. I danced around Sasha's place, legs quivering with adrenaline, every inch of me surging with life, with triumph. The grin on my face made my ears hurt. I felt a great affection for all of them, my diabolical new friends, but especially for Flynn, my comrade in endurance and lies, and I wanted to touch him, to sit close to him, to stare and stare at him and somehow confirm it really happened. We told the story over and again, from all the angles of a kaleidoscope, enlarging and diminishing and changing the colours, the same words repeated or plucked anew. I know now that this was allowed, indeed expected, the repetition, the savouring. It had its importance, consolidating the facts for those who had not been there and, for those who had, making real out of what sometimes seemed ludicrously unreal.

'God, Flynn, I was sure he'd hit you.'

'Yeah, he wanted to.'

'I couldn't believe you were waiting for us, Andy. When we walked outside and you were there, oh – '

'I asked for coffee and he told me to shut up. That's all he did, tell me to shut up. He was like a broken record.'

'When the Vicky was closed we thought they'd let us go.'

'I laughed, he told me to shut up.'

'At the Greyhound – everyone was looking at us – I kept wanting to look at you – to ask you what to say – '

'I kept wanting to *tell*.'

'And I wanted to *kill* you, Andy. You said they'd leave me alone.'

'She was great, though,' Flynn said to Andy, and I sat up straight on the arm of Flynn's chair, busting with pride.

'The cop shop was the worst,' I said. 'Being alone. I wanted to hammer on the wall and yell for you.'

They'd done to Flynn exactly what they had done to me: they told him I'd admitted everything, had cravenly dropped him in it to his chin. Sasha, Flynn and Andy seemed to regard this tactic as hilariously transparent and I was disinclined to say it had nearly fooled me.

'I kept remembering what you said in the car, *believe nothing they say*. I kept repeating it to myself, believe nothing they say, believe nothing – '

'I thought, Well, she might have admitted something, but I certainly had nothing to do with it – '

I jerked my head round to look at him, frowning. 'What did you just say?' I asked. 'Did you believe them? You believed I had confessed?'

Flynn hesitated and blinked; he said, 'Well – '

'You told me to believe nothing, yet you believed everything they said? You say it's an old trick, but you fell for it anyway?'

Flynn heard the Handbrake-ish ire rising in my voice and shifted in his chair. 'I didn't know what to think,' he mumbled.

'I didn't know what to think either, but I didn't think *that*! Jesus, Flynn.'

'Yeah, but – '

'But nothing!' I lurched away from him and flopped on the couch beside Sasha, hissing through my teeth. 'It was *me* that got us out of there, not you. I was the tough one, *I* kept to the story – *you* would have gone along with anything, so long as you got to walk in the end. Some bloody friend you turned out to be.'

'It wasn't like that – '

'Yes it was, it was exactly like that.'

'Is it just me,' Andy said mildly, 'or is this conversation getting ugly?'

For a few moments no one said anything. Jemima dropped her ears, waved her tail uncertainly. Flynn leaned forward to ash his cigarette and shot a glance at me through the rat-tails of his fringe. He knew I was faking. He knew I'd cried and that I wasn't brave. We both knew we were free because I had been pathetic, that we had sailed out the door on a wave of contempt. I went cold with shame and then with a sense of martyrdom: my methods may have been dubious, but they were nonetheless effective. 'If it hadn't been for me,' I pointed out sullenly, 'we could still be there.'

'They had nothing,' Flynn retorted darkly. 'They would have let us go.'

'They wouldn't have let us go if I'd *confessed*,' I snarled, springing up in my seat. 'If *I* had believed them, *you'd* be freezing your arse off in a prison cell right now! But I didn't believe them, and you did. I'm glad to know I can rely on you, Flynn. I'm glad to know you trust me.'

'Can we just forget it?' Andy asked. 'We're here now, and none of this matters. The conversation is going around in circles.'

'Isn't it,' mused Sasha. They were the first words he'd spoken and the three of us looked at him. Our first thought had been to come here, to Sasha's. We'd knocked on his door at midnight and he'd been undressing for bed but he didn't seem displeased or surprised to see us and made no comment about the hour. Now he sat on the edge of the couch in threadbare pyjama pants and t-shirt, his dark hair falling about his face, cutting up a mull with a pair of nail scissors. Jemima was sprawled at his feet, her chin on his toes, her eyes showing their whites to watch his every move. He hardly made it a question when he asked, 'Weren't you afraid, Louie?'

'. . . S'pose,' I said. 'A bit.'

'Then Flynn had every reason to distrust you.' He said it simply, as if commenting on the weather, and returned his attention to the mull. Flynn and I glanced sulkily at each other. I turned to Andy.

'Andy,' I said, 'did you think I would confess?'

Andy, propped against a wall with his arms around his knees, paused, and went for diplomacy. 'I didn't think anything. I just knew they'd give you a hard time.'

'. . . So you didn't trust me, either.'

Flynn drew the line abruptly. 'All right,' he sighed. 'We thought you would squeal like a piggy. We're sorry. I'm sorry. We'll know better next time. Hurry up with the mix, Sasha, you're taking all freaking night.'

My face went scarlet, I felt it. I'd pushed my grievance too far and they had lost interest. I had grated my way past humour and made myself a fool, hankering for praise like a child would, and they were not inclined toward that sort of indulgence. I'd shown myself to be petty, pulling a moot point to bits, dissecting a question that meant nothing to them. My stomach plunged with humiliation and hurt. I wanted to flee then, to never show my disgraced face again. These were not my kind of people, and I wasn't going to find a place among them.

'You were brave,' Sasha said, suddenly, to me. He put the bowl on the table and dusted his hands into it. 'If I had been there and they had told me Flynn confessed, I would have believed them.'

Flynn snorted, not looking up.

'Yes, I most certainly would.'

He was only saying it, but he usually took little notice of me, and he had never before come to my aid. So his words worked like a blessing, and all around me the ground ceased to shake; I smiled sheepishly. Looking back, I don't know what whim prompted him to favour me at that moment, other than the fact that as godfather and ringleader he could do whatever he wanted: sometimes I wonder if I could flee only when he chose to let me, rather than when I wished to do so. Regardless, while I basked in his protection I determined to abuse my position. I turned to Andy and Flynn.

'Now you have to tell me,' I said. 'You know you can rely on me now.'

'Tell you what?'

Andy and Flynn looked dour. 'That bloody Handbrake was yacking,' explained Flynn. 'Yacking about . . . stuff.'

'Stuff?' Sasha creased his brow.

'Yacking about you guys being robbers,' I chimed in. 'Stuff like that.'

'Ah.' Sasha paused, thinking. He glanced at his friends, who fixed their eyes on the furniture and refused him their help. He said, 'You know, Louie, that Elsbeth doesn't like us. She deeply resents Hastings paying attention to anyone but herself. She also has an extremely vivid imagination.'

'She didn't seem to be imagining it. Come on – tell me.'

'There's nothing to know.'

'Please, Sasha,' I wheedled, 'please tell me.'

He wavered. I knew that if I pushed him in his pampering, drowsy mood, I could coax from him what I wanted. I called upon ancient feminine wiles and gave him a blast of them. Sasha looked at me oddly.

'Why should I tell you anything?' he asked. 'I wouldn't tell you something just because you want to know, just because you don't like being left out. You have to give me a better reason than that.'

'Isn't it obvious?' I cried, because it was painfully obvious to me. I'd been good forever. I'd done nothing memorable. I'd been staid, obedient, hard-working, quiet, and above all I'd been *patient* while I waited for the world to open a door, any door, for time to make someone of me, to fill my hours, to give me a thing to think about, to bestow on me a place, a role, an importance. I saw my chance in them and their mischief, my chance of being able to say *this is where I belong*, these are my friends, this is what I mean to them, this is what I do, I live a life. I needed it, I longed for it, I truly felt I'd die if I missed this opportunity that would surely never come again.

Which would not impress *them*.

'Isn't it obvious?' I said. 'I've got a criminal mind.'

Sasha flicked up an eyebrow. Then he laughed. He laughed at me, but not unkindly: I had answered without fault. I would be their pet, I would never have power or influence, but I would learn the intricacies of the business.

They never actually told me anything; I would learn by being allowed to watch and follow and listen and imitate. I tried always to be quick and smart and useful, and I tried to stay out of the way. Some of their acquaintances would look at me suspiciously, unused to seeing a girl involved, but Sasha Johns appeared to tolerate my presence and this worked like a sedative upon them, no one said a word. The acquaintances came from everywhere and all had a purpose, an attraction that had nothing to do with personality. Most were simply cashed-up customers, regular clients who bought two or three ounces at a time and leapt at the opportunity whenever Sasha had some speed or trips or ecstasy to dispense. These people arrived at the bungalow at the strangest hours, hankering and willing to pay, and their conversation was always brief and ultra-polite. 'G'day,' some would say, nervously succinct; 'Sashy, hi!' another would yell, 'Andy, hi! Hi! – I don't know you – Louie – hi!' Sasha had no desire to make them suffer, he never made them linger while he flexed a torturous advantage over them. He gave them what they wanted, told them what he foresaw for sale on the horizon, and let them go. These were bottom-rung acquaintances, time-consumers, and thought of as small change. There were others who appeared less frequently, with more money, who talked in terms of *pounds* and *kilos*. These were the ones who got preference and quality; Sasha would occasionally go out of his way to procure for these clients what it was they needed and usually let them try before they bought. But customers are customers and friends are friends, and the most useful friends paid for nothing. Sasha's circle had friends that were locksmiths, electricians and mechanics. Sasha was friendly with drivers whose trucks had faulty rollerdoors and were prone to losing their loads. Sasha knew doctors and lawyers and accountants; most of these professionals had once been schoolmates and were still young and occasionally tentative but their friendship was nonetheless cultivated, an investment in the future.

Everyone involved in anything was paid in goods or, less preferably, cash. Sasha was scrupulously fair in the divvying up, for this was good business practice, keeping people happy and true. The obstacles of life were bartered into oblivion whenever they could be, and much of the group's time was consumed securing goods of trade. So, the accountant who jiggled the figures in Sasha's tax return got for his efforts five boxes of the imported tiles he wanted for his kitchen floor, and the locksmith who cut the key to the tile factory got the Ray-Bans he'd selected from a catalogue, but the guy who'd helped Hastings load the tiles into the truck wanted cash more than anything; Sasha rolled his eyes but emptied his wallet. There seemed to be no material good that Sasha's gang could not get their hands on: their tentacles spread until they seemed like magicians, like genies. In reality, the success of their business had its basis in the quickness of their fingers.

One day Flynn tugged my sleeve and I followed him into Sasha's bedroom. There on the bed sat a large plush teddy bear with a ribbon around its neck. It was brand-new, coming complete with tags. I had no particular liking for soft toys but I picked it up and enthused about its cuteness and Flynn seemed pleased. 'Do you want it?' he asked casually, as if the bear was incidental to the occasion, as if I'd discovered it myself in some box full of junk. 'You can have it, if you like.'

'Don't you want it?'

'Ha, no.'

'Isn't there someone else – someone's little girl – ?'

Flynn looked pained, shuffling his feet. 'You can have it, if you like.'

I took it, understanding it was always meant for me, knowing he'd seen it in some toyshop window and been struck with the idea that I would be charmed by such a thing. He'd walked in and picked it up and later a shop assistant would have noticed its absence and gone about asking everyone, 'Did you sell that bear? That bear in the window, did someone buy that?'

Every shop Sasha's friends stepped out of rang, sooner or later, with those plaintive questions.

Sometimes I would be there when they did it, but I wouldn't find out until afterwards. We'd go into a jewellery store and Andy would ask to see a particular tray of watches. He'd scan them and ask to see some more. Nothing eventful would happen, the trays would be returned safely to their shelter behind the glass. And outside in the street Andy would empty his pockets, cascading necklaces and gems. I wouldn't have seen his hands move, and neither would the man behind the counter. Such things were often sold, afterwards, to any acquaintance whose mother had a birthday coming up or who wanted to get engaged, and the monetary spoils were either divided up or stashed in the bank account kept for emergencies and large business purchases. They stole much that they had no immediate use for and sometimes I was given what they couldn't sell or exchange or no one seemed to like. For my nineteenth birthday Andy had given me some earrings I'd pointed out as nice and once I knew their favourite hobby I took to hiding them carefully, wearing them rarely.

The prince of shoplifting, however, was Flynn. Flynn, built like a mouse, stopped for identification every time he entered a pub, could walk out of a shop hefting a television. He stole video recorders and basketballs and mobile phones. One day, outside a framing shop, he spotted a print that he fancied. It was large and had a heavy frame. A week later it was rumoured to be hanging on his lounge-room wall. 'The trick of it,' he explained, 'is confidence. If you want a television, you've got to look like you went in to buy a television and that's exactly what you did, bought a television. You can't just *seem* like that's what you did, you've got to *look* like that's what you did. Don't browse in a shop aimlessly: you're there for a purpose and wandering is suspicious. Don't touch the stock, don't fiddle. Don't continuously watch the staff, don't talk to them more than you need to, don't try to be their friend. Don't let them distract you by asking if you need help, and don't you try to distract them. If you're getting too much attention, say you want to compare prices, leave and come back again. Bore them with indecision, make them hate you and want you gone. If you want a tele or a video, go to the department stores. They never know what's going on from one floor to another. Take a bag that has got the shop's name on it and tape it to the box. Get a docket and stick that to it too. If you want a telephone or a leather jacket go to a shop in a rich suburb, one that looks like it doesn't get done over very often. Choose a shopping strip where there's lots of the same kind of shop all jammed up near each other. When you go on a spree – and it's hardly worth your while unless it is a spree – always wear clean clothes, a suit if you can, have your hair brushed, look respectable. Don't wear a coat on a summer's day. If you're carrying a bag, make it a nice clean one, no brandnames everywhere.

Offer to leave it at the counter if you can do without it. Carry a bag, sometimes, for the sole purpose of leaving it behind the counter. Some places you'll need to become a familiar face before you make your move – others you can hit and run. Don't ever confuse one sort for the other. Don't waste time when you see your chance. Never panic. Never abandon your plan unless it is absolutely necessary to do so. And remember: class and confidence, class and confidence.'

He'd nod his head sagely. There was little that presented a challenge to Flynn. He stole an electric guitar one day, sliding the neck down his trousers and slipping his jumper over the rest of it, walking out of the shop with a stiff-legged limp he had not arrived with. He couldn't play the guitar; that seemed beside the point. He knew he was good at his work, but even he had his heroes: he'd get misty-eyed telling stories of the great shoplifters, those who fearlessly went where Flynn himself feared to tread. These legends stole washing machines, double beds, dining-room tables, chandeliers. By that stage I had seen enough to believe him.

I remember him arriving at Sasha's, one afternoon, with empty hands and a boiling temper. He'd lifted a pile of compact discs and, inexplicably, been hounded by the store detective. The detective had bailed him up in the street and asked to look in his bag. Flynn had defiantly refused to let him. 'You can't touch me,' he told the detective, though he knew this wasn't so. He knew that all a store detective needed was *reasonable belief* that a crime had been committed before stopping a suspect and searching a bag. *Reasonable belief*, Flynn knew, meant that the crime had to have been witnessed. Flynn had reasonable belief in his talent: he knew he hadn't been seen, that the detective had nothing, that this was a bluff meant to frighten him into making a mistake. 'Why don't you piss off,' he said.

But the detective, who was fresh-faced and determined to make a name for himself, had not accepted that invitation. He'd stalked Flynn through the city streets and lanes. When Flynn got on a tram the detective got on too. They glared at each other as they were jostled by the passengers. Flynn alighted, so did the detective. They paced through a park, keeping up a conversation.

'I know what you've got in your bag.'

'Get lost.'

'Why don't you just give up.'

'Why don't you go back to work.'

'I'm sticking with you like a fly to shit, buddy.'

Flynn veered back toward the city, sweating now. He made for the station and the crowds of people there. Losing himself, looking to the digital display for the first train anywhere. Down the escalator two gridded steps at a time, the detective bobbing through the crush behind him. A momentary diversion, a woman with a pram; Flynn reached in his bag and dumped the discs into a rubbish bin. He let the detective catch him then, and opened his empty bag. 'See?'

'You panicked,' Sasha chided, as Flynn paused in the telling.

They had stared at each other, the thief and his adversary, both panting, cheated, teeth clamping back their rage. The detective stood beside Flynn until the train arrived and Flynn stepped into it. The detective gave him the finger and Flynn smiled disdainfully through the glass.

He jumped off at the first stop and caught the next train back to the city, but the compact discs were gone. 'Some bum,' he seethed, 'had rummaged around looking for a can of beer with dregs in it. Some stinking *bum*,' he wailed, 'has my CDs!'

'That detective wasn't after you for nothing,' said Sasha. 'You made a mistake somewhere.'

They were fighting words: Flynn screamed and swore. 'A mistake! That man was insane! He was possessed!'

Sasha shrugged. 'Maybe you're starting to smell bad.'

'No. No way.' Flynn shook his head vehemently. 'No one can smell me coming.'

'You've lost your touch, then. It might be time to put you out to pasture.'

'You prick!' Flynn shrieked. 'My best work is *ahead* of me!'

'Evidently,' Sasha answered dryly.

Flynn, riled beyond description, clutched his hair and fought for breath. With all the dignity a broken man could muster he stated, 'I have not lost my touch.'

Sasha smiled tauntingly and smoked his cigarette. Flynn's green eyes narrowed on his friend.

'Fine,' he said. 'I'll prove it.'

He went back to the shop the next day, stole the same selection, and threw the discs around the bungalow like confetti at the wedding of giants.

He had his morals, though. There was nothing that irritated him more than the sight of a small store buckled and barricaded with security. Contrary to what I expected, he claimed this was the end result of petty crooks at work. He took me to a suburban hardware store to explain. 'Look around,' he said. 'What's worth stealing in here? A rake? A chisel? That bag of daffodil bulbs? Perhaps you fancy a new doormat? No, there's nothing here you want. But look at this – there's a buzzer on the door, there's mirrors on the walls, the door that leads to the back room has a big lock on it. Something funny has been going on here. There's nothing in the shop you want, so what's in that bolted back room? The safe? Probably. It wouldn't be open, you'd need an oxy-acetylene torch to get into it, and what you'd find wouldn't be worth that kind of effort. So what else is in the back room? Tin of biscuits? A hot-water urn?'

I gazed around the shop. There was a middle-aged woman behind the counter who looked like she'd been born and raised there. A young man toward the front of the shop was restocking a rack of plumbing supplies.

'The woman's handbag is in the back room,' I said. 'The man might keep his wallet in there too.'

'Exactly! Well done. Petty crooks have been sniffing around here, Louie. They've snuck into the back room and stolen the woman's purse. They've lifted the guy's keys and taken his car for a joyride. They probably did it several times before they turned these people completely paranoid. No security is enough for this place now. Wankers like that should be garrotted.'

'Why? Surely all is fair?'

'It isn't. They're vermin, thieves like that. They make life difficult for the rest of us. And where's the dignity in stealing an old lady's purse? What are you going to get – the money she's saved for her gas bill? This isn't a big company, these people get paid crap. They have to do this shitty job day after day. You're going to steal, steal from someone or something that can afford it and deserves it. Don't steal from someone as badly off as yourself. Remember what you are: you are on a rung of the ladder, not a high rung, not as high as Sasha would like to think, but you're on it, you're not the scum at the bottom. Spit on them. Let's go.'

Shoplifting was his forte, irresistible as he found an open door and the exposure that was daylight. Breaking-and-entering did not hold the same thrill for him, but it was part of his repertoire and from the day the detective stalked him he seemed determined to teach me what he knew, or at least prove to me he knew it.

'Never focus on what is *preventing* you from getting what you want,' he instructed me. We were walking home from the Vicky Greene with Andy and Hastings, and Flynn was reeling. 'Always look,' he said, 'at what is *helping* you. You have to think *positively*.'

We stopped in front of an electrical-goods store and Flynn wrapped his fingers around the bars of the metal grid that had been drawn down over the big windows. 'Look in there,' he said. 'Televisions, stereos, those groovy shiny things you make milkshakes with. But look at this horrible gate thing they've put over the windows: I don't like this *at all*. You can't kick it down, you can't cut through it in a hurry. So if I wanted all that stuff, how would I get it? This grille isn't helping me, but what is?'

I stood back and considered the dark building.

'There might be a window around the back,' Andy offered. 'A bathroom window, an office window. It would be locked, but it mightn't have bars over it.'

'It's an old shop,' observed Hastings. 'It's probably got a corrugated-iron roof. If you could get up there, you might be able to get in through the ceiling.'

Flynn sighed deeply. 'Listen to them,' he said. 'Like getting their hands dirty, they do. Not me. If *I* was going to break into this shop, I'd get a simple cordless power drill. I'd go around to the back door and I'd drill a big bastard hole straight through the lock. Take twenty seconds. That's what I'd do.'

'Me too,' said Andy.

'Yeah, me too,' agreed Hastings.

'What if an alarm goes off?' I asked.

'Turn a deaf ear,' Flynn said. 'Everyone else does.'

I liked him. Looking younger than he was, he often seemed to behave that way too. He could be shy and unnecessarily loud, and he was charmingly easy to shock: I found I could make him redden by saying the word 'breasts'. He found Sasha's serious approach to the running of the business vastly amusing, and delighted in Sasha's resulting distress, but it was always to him that Sasha turned for approval of a plan, for the sweeping up of details and the demolishing of any obstacle. I thought he liked me because I was someone new, someone he could impress with skills his friends either shared or had ceased to consider remarkable, but one day we crossed paths with his cousin and when she mistook me for his girlfriend Flynn pretended not to hear and let the mistake go by. And so did I: it seemed a harmless thing.

One drizzling afternoon he asked if I wanted to go for a drive, as I appeared to be doing nothing productive at the bungalow. In keeping with the rules of the business Flynn's car was tidy and inconspicuous, the better to be overlooked by the police. Even Hastings's big four-wheel drive was spick and span and saw, like most of its ilk, few rugged trails. The four-wheel drive was registered to and driven by Hastings but its purchase had been subsidised by the business, for the business had use for a large, spacious vehicle.

We went to Flynn's home and there he introduced me to his grandmother. I'd never imagined Flynn really living anywhere. He lurked around Sasha's and that seemed to be enough. But he lived with his grandmother, who offered me a cup of coffee, in a trim, ordinary little house, and Flynn had a bedroom which was out-of-bounds to his Nanna and which contained all his treasures. He proudly showed me a record cover signed by Iggy Pop, a dead tarantula splayed within a glass case, and a dolphin he'd created from grubby blue wax. His bedroom was messy and smelled strongly of boy. It didn't feel like he often drew the curtains. Everything was dusty. Things were lying around, flattened shoes and filled ashtrays and knotted ties, his best shirts on hangers in a cupboard without doors. The blankets on his sway-backed bed were jumbled and he made a hasty effort to straighten them, muttering, 'Oh, sorry.' And he was sorry; sorry he was so satisfied by the simple things he owned, sorry he'd let me discover this, sorry for what his bedroom said about him, sorry he had brought me here. It was a relief to be directed outside.

There was a brick garage in the garden, its door warped but tightly bolted. We stepped on mossy flagstones to reach it, followed all the way by a mewling calico cat. The garage had sheets of iron nailed over its windows but, inside, it was ablaze with brightness. At one end of the garage were twelve tall marijuana plants growing in a bed of fibrous, waterlogged material. They were thriving, bushy, glossily green, their weight supported by a network of strings that pulled them upright and kept them from sprawling. Arranged around the walls were trays of young, delicate plants, their leaves small as a baby's hand, their jagged fingers spread. The walls themselves were covered in mouldy black plastic, down which droplets coursed sluggishly. At the other end of the garage, mature plants were dangling upside-down from the ceiling, hanging out to dry. Their foliage was dull and crispy and the floor beneath them was littered with parched, shattered leaves.

'Watch your head,' Flynn told me, and we ducked between the great lights that were suspended from the ceiling, their huge bulbs reflecting heat and light off the silver shades. The room was breathlessly humid and pans of water were placed everywhere to help make it more so.

'Do you – sell this?'

'Most of it.'

I nodded, staring about in wonder. I'd never seen so much greenery in such a small space. There was a low, constant droning noise and it came from the pumps that circulated water around the plant roots; it was a surprisingly lulling noise, and it made you need to speak quietly. Flynn had gone to work at a table piled high with the driest plants, clipping off buds and dropping them into plastic bags at his feet.

'Do you make a lot of money from it?'

He gave a little cough of laughter. 'Shit, yeah,' he said. 'Look at it, Louie.'

'No, not them – you. You.'

'Oh.' He looked around and shrugged. 'No, not really. Not me.'

'But you grow them,' I said. 'You do all the work.'

Flynn returned his attention to the table. 'I don't do much,' he replied. 'They look after themselves, mostly. The timers tell them when it's night and when it's day. I just make sure they're not thirsty. That's not hard. Once it's grown, that's when the work starts. It's got to be weighed and bundled up. It's got to be sold. That's a hassle. I don't get involved in that.'

The cat was at a gap in the door, one golden eye focused on us and darting up and down like a searchlight. It forced a paw into the space and waggled it, meowing. Flynn ran a hand through the brittle foliage, crumpling the leaves between his fingertips.

'I don't mind looking after them,' he said. 'I like watching them grow. I like talking to them.'

'And beheading them.'

'We all,' he said solemnly, 'must earn our keep.'

'Doesn't your grandmother *know* about this? This industry in her backyard?'

'Probably. She never says anything. She's good.'

He filled the bags with buds and leaf and then produced some papers and rolled a neat joint. I sat on a wonky stool and Flynn sat cross-legged on the floor. The cat rattled the door, yowling with frustration, but we smoked in silence, passing the joint back and forth.

'That's why I like living here,' he said eventually. 'Nan doesn't mind what I do. She doesn't bother me. I can come and go, do whatever I like. I could live at home if I wanted to, with my dad, but I wouldn't have – all this. This set-up, this privacy.'

He waved at the room and its contents and I said I understood. Later, struggling to make conversation with Sasha, I commented on the story and he laughed grimly. 'Yeah, right,' he said.

'What?'

'Flynn can't live *at home*. The only home he's got is the one he is living at now.'

Sasha was dividing up the dope Flynn had put in the bags. He was using a pair of pewter scales to weigh it up an ounce at a time. I was unsealing plastic sandwich bags and holding them out, gape-mouthed, for the dope to be tipped into when the scales hovered even. No one but me found this task interesting and the others were outside kicking a football around the slushy garden. Chopper, the bull-terrier owned by Hastings, would sometimes snatch the ball and run and we could hear Andy laugh when this happened, and the bellowing of Hastings.

'Flynn has lived with his grandmother almost all his life,' Sasha continued, snapping off a stem and dropping it in the ashtray. 'His mother is dead. I think she killed herself. He never talks about her. He's never told me what happened, how she died. Just says, *Well, she died.* So I gather she topped herself. Flynn lived with his father but his dad was a boozer, a useless prick. One morning he told Flynn he was going out and when Flynn asked him where he was going, he said, *I'm going to see a man about a dog*. Flynn was only a kid, in primary school. He was only eight. He didn't know what that means, seeing a man about a dog, he didn't know he was being told to mind his own business. He waited all day for his dad to come home with the dog, and when he rang his grandmother to ask how to cook himself some dinner, she came over and found him sitting there with newspaper spread out on the kitchen floor and a bowl and a blanket all ready, waiting for the dog.'

Jemima, curled on the couch beside Sasha, woke up and yawned. She nuzzled into the crook of his arm and Sasha smiled, patting her broad snout. 'Flynn's been living with his grandmother ever since,' he said. 'I don't think he's ever owned a dog.'

He sat forward, drew the scales closer and added, without looking at me, 'That's Flynn's problem, you know. His whole life is imaginary. He'll never actually go anywhere or do anything. He just lives in dreams.'

Alexandra hardly ever smokes, she says she doesn't want wrinkles or cancer either, but she shakes a cigarette out of my packet with a glance that asks my permission and at the same time thanks me for it. I make sure the pack stays near her, in case she wants another. It's getting hot in the loft, and the clay smell is getting thicker. I can feel sweat between my fingers and toes.

Kate, who's lying on the floor with her head propped in her hands, seems to find no fault with the story so far, but she says that she didn't see much of Daniel after that first night at the pub, because she didn't like him. She went out with the pair of them a few times but then she dug her heels in and for the next few months she'd see less of Alexandra, refusing to go out if Daniel was going to be there, curling her lip if Daniel became a topic. So Alexandra would come to feel she was alone, afraid that, if she talked to Kate about anything, Kate might say, *I told you so*.

'What sort of friend do you think I am?' Kate asks angrily.

Alex shrugs; she can't help what she felt at the time. Now that she has to leave Kate behind in the telling she looks a little nervous, like she's setting off to some wilderness she'd rather not go into and possibly may not survive. I wonder how closely she'll stick to the truth, now she is unescorted – if she'll back off, when the scenery gets sinister.

If Alexandra went home with whatever man she chose, she had no problem getting rid of them as well. Most of them were disposed of after a single night, and she fended off their ensuing phonecalls and pleading with kind but firm words. She never refused their calls, never got her mother to say she was busy, never left it to them to work out that their attentions were no longer required. This sort of thing had been done to her, and she knew it was cruel. Often she made it clear right from the start that the arrangement was temporary. Sex, as far as Alex was concerned, was hilarious, and didn't really mean anything. She treated it more lightly than she treated a serious conversation. She could not understand why people attached such heavy importance to an act that was so frequently funny. She was, however, no floozy. She valued herself and she always cared, at least a bit, for the guys she picked up. She was, like everyone everywhere, hopeful that she would meet someone she could adore all her life and she would cast off her gallivanting when he appeared, but until he did she would keep herself amused. She had no intention of settling for second best. She would rather go without, than be with a second best.

When she wakes that first morning she discovers that she's enjoyed her time with Daniel. She's been known, in the past, to creep from a bed and scuttle from a house, waving down a taxi while struggling into her clothes, swearing to mend her ways. This time, however, she's content to nestle into the blankets and go back to sleep. Daniel might wake up and tell her he is busy, reeking of the desire to be rid of her, and though she will accept his decision as proof that the alcohol had deranged her and he is, in reality, a fool, she will be disappointed.

When he does wake, he isn't foolish. He makes breakfast and brings it to her in bed, toast and hot chocolate and tablets for her hangover, all set out on a tray with a rose. He's snipped the flower from a neighbour's plant, having snuck into the street in his dressing-gown.

She knows not to overstay her welcome but accepts the offer of a shower, drying herself with a clean white towel. He talks to her through the door but doesn't invite himself into the bathroom. He makes coffee and while it brews she sits outside in the cold winter sun. She starts to hum, because she is happy, and after a moment she hears the sound of a guitar accompanying her through the tune. She looks in the window and it's him, playing the guitar. He can play the guitar. It makes her heart pound.

He is a student, studying law. He's done other things, he's drifted the same as everyone, but now he has decided his calling is to be a lawyer. 'Why?' she asks, and he says, 'I hate seeing people get away with things they shouldn't. I hate it that some people don't have a voice to defend themselves. I want to see justice done.'

'How noble.'

'I'm not doing it to be noble,' he says. 'It's what I want to do with my life. I'm thinking of applying for a position in the country.'

'Why?'

He shrugs. 'City firms want someone young, someone who's gone straight from school to university to work. They don't want you to have any experience in life. It makes it harder for them to train your mind into what they want it to be. And no one wants to work in the country. So it's probably my best chance of getting a job.'

'I've always wanted to live in the country,' Alexandra tells him. 'I want a cottage and some goats and a pony, and a studio that looks over miles and miles of hills and trees. That's what I've wanted all my life.'

'Aren't you happy, living here?'

'I'm not unhappy. But it's what I want. I want it more and more as time goes by. You can't help what you want.'

'Why don't you do it, then?'

She crinkles her nose. 'I'm not brave enough to go alone

and no one will come with me. They think I'm weird, to want it at all.'

'Well,' he says, 'you could come with me. We could go together.'

She looks at him. 'OK,' she says.

They both know it is only a joke, an agreement feeble and offhand, but it changes something between them. It becomes a solid thing, as if they've exchanged gifts.

He doesn't telephone the next day, or the next, but then he does so, and she is giggly with relief.

'So,' says Kate, 'you'd known him a single day and already you were moving in together. To the country. In a cottage.'

Alexandra winces. 'I know how it sounds. It sounds insane. But he was the first guy I'd ever met who wanted the same thing as I did.'

'He didn't *want* it, it was the only choice he *had* – '

'Let her tell the story,' I say. Kate slumps on her elbows.

His law course keeps him busy and he is at university for long periods of the day; three evenings a week he dons a beige uniform and spends a few hours cleaning offices for spending-money. Her own time has few demands on it: the pottery shop is not like a real job, it's just like what she does for fun at home, in her own studio. So she has lots of time to think. In those early days her thoughts are consumed by him: she sees a suit in a window and wonders if navy is his colour, she hears a joke and itches to tell him. She goes out with Kate sometimes, and Kate doesn't yet hate Daniel as much as she eventually will, and when Kate sees Alexandra's thoughts drift to Daniel, she thinks it's funny. 'I think you're in love,' she says, and laughs.

Alexandra begins to think, more seriously, about a house in the country.

He telephones most afternoons, and if he can stall the writing of an essay and he isn't going cleaning he asks her to come around. He lives alone, for his housemate has gone overseas for a year, and it's easier for her to go to his house than to invite him over to hers. He worries about her driving and imagines crashes, thugs enraged swinging sledgehammers, doing in her lights: he seems determined that a disaster will befall her and he encourages her to stay in the house even when he's not there, rather than tempt such trauma. By the time they have been going out for three weeks, she is at his house almost every day and he has given her the spare key.

Except, he never says they are *going out*: their relationship had begun casually, and this seems to prevent him from taking it seriously. He has a few friends he's met at university and when she and he go out with them he pays her no special attention, leaving her to manage as best she can. It grates on her, this lack of recognition. When she mentions it to him, he growls, 'Jesus, Alex, grow up.'

There are other things, too – only a month into their relationship she has started to worry that she bores him, for she often finds herself scouting for conversation. She discovers they have almost nothing in common: he has no interest in art, he doesn't really like socialising, they don't appreciate the same TV shows. Few things amuse him or even make him happy, and she devotes a lot of energy trying to jolly him from his dourness. Sometimes he gives in to her efforts; sometimes he takes her playfulness for a lack of concern about his troubles. She can never predict which way he will go. She finds he isn't particularly interested in sex: he will sometimes, impatiently, avoid her touch. In her arms, he keeps a silence that's eerie. Sometimes, afterwards, he steps out of bed and fills the bathroom sink to wash the bits of him that have touched her most closely.

'You have got to be *kidding* me!' The words almost explode out of Kate, who flings herself off the floor and gapes at Alex. 'He used to wash his *dick* in the *sink* after you'd have *sex* with him?'

I feel myself blushing, so look harder at the floor. Kate is laughing, but not merrily, and Alexandra's laughing too, but it's a choking kind of sound. 'What did you do?' Kate asks. 'What did you *say*? Weren't you *insulted*?'

'I couldn't decide whether I was insulted or not,' Alex says. 'It sounds insulting when I describe it now, but then it just seemed – I don't know – like something that was different, but forgivable, not worth making a fuss about. Everything – everything seemed like that. No point in making a fuss because what's done is done. Getting upset wasn't going to change anything.'

We look at each other, and we all seem to sink, then – Kate to the floor, Alex into her chair. 'I'd have changed things,' Kate snarls: she makes a mangling motion with her hands.

One night, lying beside her, he says, 'I don't need a girlfriend.'

She thinks she hasn't heard right and moves closer. 'Huh?'

'I don't need a girlfriend,' he repeats.

'Oh,' she says, hollowly.

'I don't need friends or a girlfriend.' He states it like an announcement.

'That's not a very nice thing to say,' she says softly. He turns his head to look at her.

'No one *needs* friends or *needs* to go out with anyone,' he tells her. 'That's just bullshit.'

She doesn't know what to make of that. The terrible things he says seem to be directed at everyone, at the whole anonymous world with himself included, so she can hardly protest – yet their points seem sharpened specially for her, and they hurt.

Still, if there are things Alexandra doesn't like about him, there are other things that she does, and this mix of pros and cons tempts her to think that the relationship is normal. As time passes, his hair grows, and she thinks he looks divine, she can stare at him and be amazed that such a handsome thing is hers. He cooks meals for her, lugging home bags of groceries and spending hours at the stove, shooing her away if she tries to help, cutting up an apple for her to eat while she waits. When they go for walks, he takes her hand and draws her close; in a crowd he shepherds her protectively, taking knocks and bumps himself. She falls off her bike one day and the small injury to her elbow is treated as life-threatening. If, in her absence, he goes for milk or takes a shower, he leaves the phone off the hook, so that if she telephones she will think he is home and ring again soon. When he knows she is coming over he waits on the doorstep and she sees pleasure on his face when he finally spots her car. She recognises that look on the faces of others, couples in the park, couples on the street, and she thinks, *I am one of you: I am loved*. They've been going out only two months when the subject of children comes up and they find themselves arguing over what to call a child that doesn't even exist; when they hear themselves they go immediately quiet and glance bashfully at each other.

And they talk about the country.

He starts to apply for positions, for this is his final year at school, and she helps him write and print his résumé and then seal the copies in envelopes destined for townships everywhere. They agree they are not fussy about which town they should live in, as long as it is small, as long as it is green. He says she can keep anything she wants: a pony, a pig, a calf. They envisage a vegetable garden and a shed where she will work. He seems charmed by the idea of coming home each night to find her there, in the house they will first rent and then buy. She loves it when they talk about this, and she loves him. She imagines what it might be like to grow up in the country, and to grow old there as well. She stuffs résumés into envelopes and all her hopes go with them. It seems extraordinary that she's met him, crossed his path so easily, the one person in the world who can help fulfil her single, lifelong dream. She puts this to him and he says, 'It was because of my lucky coin.'

'*My* lucky coin,' she corrects. 'Remember, you gave it to me.'

'I didn't give it to you,' he says.

She pauses. 'Yes,' she says tentatively. 'You gave it to me. You insisted I take it.'

'That's exactly what I said, *take it*. I didn't say you could *have* it.'

She had thought he was in a good mood, but his mood can plunge in a moment, and the haul back up can sometimes take days. 'It's the same thing,' she says quietly.

'No it isn't – it isn't at all. I could say, take that plate when you go to the kitchen, but it doesn't make the plate *yours*, does it? It's in your possession, but it isn't yours.'

Alexandra shakes her head. 'That's ridiculous – '

'No it's not – you're just saying that because you know I'm right.'

She stares at him. She detests his bad moods. She loathes the fact that she always seems responsible for them, yet she almost never knows what she's done wrong. Whatever she says now, the damage is already done. 'Fine,' she sighs, 'whatever. It's yours.'

'That's right.' He folds his arms and looks at the television. After a bit he says, 'Actually, give it back. I want the coin back, Alex.'

She doesn't answer, pretending to watch the TV. From the corner of her eye she can see him staring at her. He says nothing for a while. Then, 'Well, where is it?'

'Where is what?'

'My dollar.'

She looks at him. 'You know,' she says, 'I hate this trait of life, how a normal situation can suddenly turn ugly and irrational. A minute ago we were talking about the country, and now we're fighting over a coin. It's absurd.'

'What's absurd? Who's fighting? I'm just asking for something that's mine. You know I keep everything.'

And he does: he souvenirs everything. When they go to the movies he keeps the ticket stubs; he keeps the notes she writes him and the doodles she draws on his telephone pad. He preserves these things in a scrapbook; other, past girlfriends have pages in it too. 'You can't have the dollar,' she says. 'I'm sorry. I spent it. I spent it before I knew you liked to keep things.'

'What did you buy?'

'A chocolate, I think.'

He stares at her severely, pressing his lips together. 'You shouldn't be eating chocolate.'

'Why not?'

'It's bad for you. Bad for your skin. You'll get pimples.'

She opens her mouth and suddenly can't speak. She will not allow this conversation to continue. 'I'm trying to watch the television,' she says.

'Don't change the subject, Alex.'

She tosses her head and glares at him. 'What, exactly, *is* the subject, Daniel?'

'I want my dollar.'

'I *told* you, I've *spent* it. You'll never see it again because I've *spent* it.'

'You wouldn't have.'

'*Why not*?'

'Because it is important to me. It's important to both of us.'

'How? How is a stupid coin *important* to us?'

'It has meaning!' he squawks. 'If you never thought it did, what are you doing here?'

And he seems overcome with a kind of furious hysteria: he grabs her handbag and starts rifling through it. 'Daniel!' she yells; when he tips the contents onto the carpet she roars his name but he doesn't listen, doesn't stop or look up. He scatters her keys, her makeup, her address book and her tissues, he opens her wallet and shakes out the change. He unzips the bag's compartments and stuffs his hands in there, he pulls the cards from the slips inside her wallet. 'Stop it, Daniel,' she orders, not screaming it as she wants to because to scream would be to recognise reality in a scene she can not believe she's seeing. But he does not stop: he rummages on the floor, throwing things aside, and when he kneels on her hairbrush and the handle breaks with a snap she snatches up her bag and hisses, 'What's the matter with you?'

He looks into her eyes, his arms hanging limp. His gaze seems cloudy, as if part of him's not there to appreciate the view. She frowns, asks, 'Daniel? Are you all right?'

He raises his hands and shoves her, hard, in the chest.

She stumbles backwards but manages to keep her feet. He hasn't really hurt her; she is too stunned to be hurt. Daniel, too, seems stunned; his hands have not dropped completely to his side. 'I'm sorry,' he croaks, and bursts into tears.

Kate gets to her feet suddenly, and we look at her. She goes to the window, taking chipped little steps like a bird or a wind-up toy. 'What's the matter?' asks Alex.

'Nothing,' she says.

I look at her, and then I look back to Alexandra. 'I don't

care,' I say. 'I don't care if we're in trouble. I'm glad.'

Alex smiles, at me.

She gazes at him, speechless, completely gutted of inspiration.

'Sorry sorry sorry,' he burbles, rocking back and forth like a ball. 'I'm so sorry – '

'It's all right,' she murmurs, knowing that it isn't. He, too, seems to disagree, and shakes his head violently.

'It's not!' he weeps. 'It's not all right!'

He hunches and cries, chanting apologies. Alexandra looks around helplessly, and eventually crouches beside him. 'Daniel,' she soothes, 'don't cry. I'm not hurt.'

'I didn't mean it – I didn't – '

'I know.'

'I just – I don't know what's happening with us – '

'How do you mean? What's wrong, Dan?'

He drags in breaths and heaves them out again. 'What are we doing?' he asks. 'Where are we going? This all seems so – serious – we weren't supposed to have a relationship, Alexandra, it was just meant to be fun, but now we're talking about going away, living together, we don't even know each other – '

It is the first time she feels the yank as her dream is pulled from under her. Her face turns very red. 'I'm sorry,' she says. 'I'll go – I'll go – '

'But I don't want you to go! I don't!'

'Well, then, I won't – '

'But what if I want you to? What if I want you to go, one day?'

'Then – I'll go – '

She feels utterly hurt, so purposefully crushed that she sits on the floor. She does not want it to be over: she's clinging to her dream with a ferocity that can survive any torture. Daniel recovers slowly, wiping his face with his palms, smearing the snot and repentance away. Eventually he sits up, his blue eyes down. He flattens out a few stray tears. 'I feel like I've promised you so much,' he says. 'I'm afraid you'll be disappointed.'

'It doesn't matter,' she says, she lies.

'I'm not a very nice person.'

'Oh, you're OK.'

'I haven't even got any money. I can't take you anywhere. I can't buy you anything. I've got rent to pay this week and I haven't even got that, for God's sake . . .'

Money is something she knows: she knows it as a simple thing and of little importance. Money problems have always been solved with a twitch of her fingers. Her father writes a cheque and she kisses his cheek. 'Then let me help you,' she says. 'You've got enough to worry about.'

'No.'

'Why not? It makes sense. If you're worried, I'm worried, and then neither of us is happy.'

He glances at her and she recognises the droopy expression

he wears when trying to look endearing. 'I'd pay you back,' he says.

'I know.'

He sniffs and pauses, and laughs gruffly. 'I hate myself, Alex.'

'And I hate you, Dan, but that doesn't mean I'll let you be thrown onto the street.'

The next day she gives him a cheque for the amount he needs. She senses the scorn that would meet her decision so she never tells anyone that she's given him money, not her family, certainly not Kate. She knows she will seem to have acted stupidly, that no one will understand she gave Daniel money not because she was careless or gullible but because it settled her dream beneath her feet again, it gave her back her hopes.

He unfolds the cheque when it's safely in his hands, and he studies it. 'I don't know how long it will take to repay you. It could take a few weeks. Maybe even a few months.'

'That's all right,' she says. 'No hurry.'

'No hurry . . .' He grins, showing teeth. 'You know what?'

'No. What?'

'I am guaranteed to know you,' he says, 'for as long as it takes to repay you this money, and that could be months. I'll know you for months.'

She smiles, and he comes to her and wraps his arms around her. 'I'm sorry,' he says.

'I've forgiven you.' She rests her head on his shoulder. 'I love you, Dan,' she says suddenly. He laughs, and hugs her tight.

'I four-letter-word you, too,' he says.

Winter ended, but it didn't. It held on into spring and the gales of October could not blow it away. The university year ended and while I studied for my exams I shivered, hands clamped beneath my thighs. My friendship with Andy and his associates had distracted me, and I'd been studying in fits and starts: I borrowed Andy's old lecture notes to try to fill the gaps. I promised myself that next year I would do better – attend more classes, spend time in the library – but *next* year meant nothing to me, not really. I had no sense of a future at all. I wasn't working toward something on my horizon, for my life was horizon-free. I lived, instead, hour by hour, and I liked it that way, and I liked it because I sensed things would not be that way forever.

Cassy came to visit me and said, 'I haven't seen you for months, Louie.'

I'd been sorting my study notes when she arrived and I turned back to them now. 'A couple of months,' I corrected.

'What have you been doing?'

'. . . Lots,' I said. 'Heaps. I've been so busy. School – you know.'

She did know: Cassy was a photographer and was studying at the College of Arts. She liked to photograph tiny creatures and blow them up huge, and you'd wonder how you ever stepped on such a thing. She wasn't lazy, like me, and she did not drift purposelessly: she'd wanted all her life to be a photographer and she invested all her energy in her work. She sat on my bed and looked around. I'd recently thrown out my posters and she commented, 'Your room looks bare.'

'I like it like this. All that stuff – it was kid's stuff. I'm trying to get rid of rubbish.'

'But you'd had some of them for years – '

'Well, that was the point,' I said, impatiently. I shuffled the papers and rearranged them until I'd made a disordered, satisfying mess, and laid down my hands. I glanced at Cassy, who was flipping idly through my music collection. She was wearing the type of clothes she always wore, the kind you knew her mother had chosen for her. She wore her hair the way she'd worn it for years, a fine blunt bob that swung limply around her ears. A year at the College, where she would have met the most radical of artists, had had no discernible effect on her presentation. I didn't care what she looked like, but I resented her imperviousness. 'You don't like change, do you?' I said, and she lifted her eyes.

'I like it when it's for the better,' she replied.

I turned to my desk, dumped a paperweight on the pages. She was wearing perfume, the dainty one or two dabs that she would have been told was enough, and the smell was irrationally offensive to me. I didn't want her here, and I could think of nothing to say to her. I felt guilty about that, and slightly sad, but I still wanted her gone.

'Cassy,' I said, 'let's go outside and have a joint.'

Her round eyes blinked, and blinked again. She said, 'Dope, you mean? You've got dope?'

I yanked open the desk drawer and produced a plastic bag of it. She held out a hand and I passed it to her for inspection and she stared at it, fascinated. 'When did you start smoking dope?'

'Oh, you know. Months ago.'

'Do your parents know?'

I lounged against the table, casually debauched. 'You know what they're like,' I said. 'They'd carry on, and on and on. I go to the park and smoke it there.'

She had so far shown none of the anticipated signs of alarm: she hadn't dropped the dope and scurried off, never to return. She opened the bag and sniffed, drew away with crinkled nose. 'OK, I'll try it,' she said. 'Don't laugh if it makes me cough.'

I goggled at her; I might have goggled all day if the telephone hadn't rung and my little brother hadn't called out for me. It was Andy on the phone. 'What are you doing?' he asked, and I told him I was doing nothing.

'Can you come to Sasha's? Right now?'

'I've got a visitor – '

'No, you have to come. We need you.'

'Well, then,' I said, 'OK.'

'Come as fast as you can.'

'What's happened?'

'Nothing, yet,' he said, 'but it will.'

It would take me forty minutes to walk the distance so I told Cass we'd have to raincheck the drugs and coaxed my mum into driving me to Sasha's. My mother was impressed at the sight of the Johns' gracious residence and remarked upon the standard of people with whom I was now mingling. Despite the lift, I had not arrived in time. The Handbrake had beaten me and the walls of the bungalow were shuddering.

'You pathetic bastards!' she was screaming. 'I hate you! You fat-head cretinous bastards, I *hate* you!'

Her abuse was not up to its usual razorblade cuttingness and there were tears in her lashes. Andy, Sasha and two strangers were sitting very still in their seats and Sasha had blood smeared over his shirt. Only their eyes moved to register my arrival, as if anything more would be interpreted as provocation. 'What's going on?' I asked. 'Elsbeth, what's the matter?'

The fire was spluttering inside her; her whole body sagged and she looked at me through misery. 'David is in hospital,' she mumbled emptily, and I thought for a moment she would fall. I put an arm round her shoulders and looked past her to the others.

'What's going on?' I asked again, and they just looked surly. The strangers, I saw, were white-faced and longing to leave. She'd gouged them out before I got there and the four of them were thoroughly, huffishly stung. I turned away and said to her, 'Come outside, with me.'

She wiped her tears as we walked through the garden and Jemima loped over to be with us. There was a bench beneath a maple tree and we mopped the raindrops from it and sat down. We could see the bungalow from there, but no sound or movement came from within. I could imagine them rolling eyes at each other, smirking, swearing under their breath, trotting out the spiteful lines that guys use against absent girls. I fiddled in my bag for a tissue and Elsbeth pressed it to her damp face. 'Is he all right?' I asked.

'I don't know. Sasha says he is. He has to be in hospital overnight.'

'He must be all right then. If it's only overnight.'

Elsbeth sniffed and didn't reply. She reached down to stroke Jemima's silky coat. 'You're a nice dog,' she whispered. 'You're a nice old dog.'

'Do you want to go to the hospital? I'll go with you, if you want.'

'No, I'll be OK. Thanks.' She straightened, and considered the bungalow. 'He'd better be all right,' she added, menacingly.

'They wouldn't have said – '

'They'd *say* anything,' she snapped. 'They'd do anything. Anything that suits them. Always have. Hastings is just the same. I asked him not to go today, he went anyway. I should be laughing that he got hurt. I should be *laughing*.' She kicked the ground so savagely that a clump of grass and soggy dirt got tossed into the air. She frowned at the damage she'd done, used her heel to hide the hole in the earth.

'You really despise them, don't you,' I remarked. I wondered where she found the stamina, in her slim ladylike frame, for such contempt.

'You've only seen them being polite and perfect,' she replied. She turned her face to me and there were black smudges of eyeliner all over her cheeks. 'You've only had them be nice to you. They call me *the Handbrake*. That's how they try to get at me. They can't touch me any other way. Do you think they're being polite about me in there?'

I said nothing, and Elsbeth grimaced. She looked back at the bungalow and sniffed fiercely. 'Shoplifting,' she said, 'selling dope, robbing stuff. No one cares much about that sort of thing, it doesn't really matter. People laugh at that type of thing. But I have seen Sasha take a guy by the hair and smash that guy's head against a brick wall until the guy's nose was pulverised in a mash across his face and blood was just gushing out. Sasha didn't stop, though. He kept slamming the guy against the wall until all the guy's teeth were broken. Sasha was happy, then. You piss him off, you lose your teeth. Your *teeth*, for God's sake.'

She looked at me, but I was staring at the grass.

'Flynn,' she continued. 'I've seen Flynn drag a guy from a car and whack him with a golf club. He hit him on the shins and the guy fell on the road. Flynn just lifted that club and crashed it down on the guy's ribs. He could have snapped the guy's spine. He hit and hit, on the shoulders and feet and elbows, and then when he got bored with that he kicked him, hard, in the head. Then he just tucked the club under his arm and walked away, dusting off his hands.'

Jemima had fetched her tennis ball and dropped it at our feet and now stood tense and impatient, glancing now and then at the ball to remind us about it. Elsbeth picked it up and threw it and the dog dashed away. 'A friend of theirs once shot some guy,' she told me. 'He went to prison for that. Sasha's taking care of the gun. It's in his cupboard, go and look. Another friend was charged with grievous bodily harm after he ruptured some man's spleen. I won't tell you,' she said, 'what I've seen Andy do.'

'Worse?' I asked thinly.

'Not *worse*, I suppose. He's only as bad as the rest of them.'

It was cool out in the garden and I wrapped my arms around myself. 'They must have reasons?' I suggested finally. 'That guy – Sasha must have had a reason – '

'They're violent,' Elsbeth said simply. 'They've always got a reason and sometimes the reason is that they're in the mood to be violent. Got to get rid of that energy somehow. Why not knock the crap out of someone, that'll do it . . . Have you ever heard a thighbone crack? I have. So has Sasha. It made him laugh.'

I sat back, stunned. 'What does Hastings do?' I asked, pointedly. Hastings was the tallest, the heaviest, the strongest; surely his hands were the most bloody.

'David does whatever they tell him. He's the biggest moron of them all. But David, at least, doesn't do it simply because he feels like hurting someone. He doesn't take someone outside because they're boring him, or they've said something to annoy him, or they've accidentally looked at him sideways.'

'They don't hit – girls, though, do they?'

'I've seen Sasha look at me like he wants to kill me,' she said, and smiled crookedly. 'But I don't think they would hit a girl. That wouldn't fit their image of themselves. They pretend they're gentlemen. Gentlemen criminals. Sasha can charm the socks off anyone. It makes me want to throw up.'

I stayed silent, finding nothing to say. I had seen Sasha on the train with a blind man, I'd heard the heart-rending pride Flynn took in his waxy dolphin, I'd been touched by Andy's amateurish wrapping of my birthday present: I found it hard to believe we were talking about the same people. It occurred to me that Elsbeth might be making things up as she went along. She bore them a grudge, the denigrated Handbrake, and she was prone to exaggeration in everything she did.

But, inside, I knew what she was saying was true, and I believed her. I'd met their acquaintances. I'd been told to leave the bungalow and go home, for reasons I could not fathom. I'd been excluded on occasions and Andy would not tell me what I had missed. I'd heard conversations go cold when I entered the room. I'd seen looks on their faces that made them, for a moment, difficult to recognise. Shoplifting was their game; they did other things, things I was never going to find out about. They broke people's bones. They made weapons out of golf clubs. They did things that landed them, and those they encountered, in hospital. And I thought, does this bother me? And I thought *no*, it doesn't. On the contrary, I felt a certain perverse conceit in having friends who were dangerous, as if I were mixing in the company of wolves. I was sure they had reasons for what they did, I was sure whoever they did it to deserved to have it done. They wouldn't deign to explain and justify every detail of their activities to the Handbrake. I knew I'd be more watchful now, but, as long as I was safe, there was no denying the attraction of it. And I thought: what sort of person does that make me?

'How come you hang around with them,' I asked, 'if you hate them so much?'

'I don't hang round with them,' she corrected testily. 'Hastings hangs round with them. I hang round with Hastings and Hastings hangs round with them.'

The screen door of the big house opened and a woman stepped past it, a stately woman in a long purple dress. She carried a pot of flowers which she placed on the decking beside the pool, and she fluffed out the leaves prettily. She saw us in the distance, shaded her eyes and waved, and we waved back. 'Sasha's mum,' Elsbeth told me. 'She doesn't know what her precious boy is like.'

'What happened today, anyway?'

'David got his arm slashed.'

'Not – stabbed?'

Elsbeth shook her head. 'They smashed a window to get into a factory. He cut himself on the glass. He needed seventeen stitches.'

'But he's in hospital?'

'He lost a lot of blood.'

'Oh.'

'I know why, too. They didn't take him to hospital as soon as he hurt himself. They made him go and sit in the truck while they did whatever they wanted to do at the factory. Then they dropped him off at the hospital on the way home. They made him wait in the car and bleed and bleed.'

She shot a bitter glance across the garden, to where the glossy green four-wheel drive was parked. 'I hate that fucking truck,' she said. 'The business owns half of it. Sasha won't sell that share to us. He knows that, if he did, Hastings wouldn't have to come every time Sasha whistled.'

'But he would,' I said. 'He would come when Sasha whistled, anyway.'

'I know,' she said.

She continued to gaze at the four-wheel drive, throwing the ball absently when Jemima brought it to her.

'Years ago,' she said, 'Hastings and I went camping for a weekend. I remember it was really, really hot when we were driving there, and I had a hangover and we were both in the foulest moods. We're driving along and I'm bitching and he's bitching, I'm saying *Let's go home, I don't want to go camping*, and he's saying *We're going camping, you said you wanted to go camping, we've got the tent*, blah blah blah, we were at each other's throats the whole way. And then all of a sudden the car starts to buck and stall and finally it just stops dead, in the middle of this empty road, nothing but trees and scrub all around. Hastings opened the bonnet and steam came billowing out. The engine was completely rooted. So I start yelling at him and he starts walking away. *Where are you going?* I ask, and he says, *We can't stand here forever, can we?* So I follow him, screaming my head off. It was so hot I thought we'd die out there, on some road to nowhere. I reckon we walked for ten miles. It felt like a hundred. We were sweating and not talking. We found this old service station and I went to the toilets and filled the sink and just put my head in this water, this brown disgusting water. We had a rest and then we started walking again. David had bought a bottle of Coke and it got so warm, it was like syrup. Finally a car came along and David put his thumb out and the car stopped. I thought for a moment it wasn't going to and I nearly threw myself on the road in front of it. I'd rather have died than walked any further.'

She paused, her crimson lips curving at the memory. 'We got a lift all the way into the town,' she continued. 'I was looking out the window as we drove along, thinking, *I would have died here – no, here – no, here*. When we got to the town David said, *Fuck it, we're staying at the motel*. So we stayed the night at this expensive motel but it was worth it, there was a pool and the pub was just around the corner. When we'd cooled down we felt better, we started to think it was hilarious, we went to the pub and had a counter meal and it was a really good night, in the end . . . but it had been hell, walking all that way. It had been utter . . . hell.'

There was movement at the bungalow: the strangers came out, accompanied by Sasha, got into their cars and drove away. Sasha waved them goodbye, then looked across the lawn to us. He had changed out of his bloodied shirt and I wondered why he hadn't done so before Elsbeth had seen it, if he simply hadn't had the opportunity or if he had deliberately intended to torment. Elsbeth's eyes darted away from him and she pawed self-consciously at her face.

'The next morning,' she said, 'Hastings and I walked through town and we came to this tiny car-yard. It was hardly even proper, it only had two cars sitting in this little concrete yard, a few faded streamers and flags. Hastings walks up to this yellow car and starts looking it over. The man comes out of his hut and starts telling us what a good car it is, how it's got air-conditioning and everything. Hastings asks how much it costs and lifts up the bonnet. *Can we take it for a test drive?* he asks, and the guy says, *Sure.* So Hastings and I get into this car and drive off. I thought he was seriously thinking about buying it, that we were honestly going on a five-minute test drive. But then we're driving and driving, we drive right out of town and Hastings keeps driving, turns on the air-conditioner and the radio, starts singing along. Driving, driving, and it just occurs to me, *We're stealing this car. We're driving home in this stolen yellow car.* It seemed so – bizarre – I didn't even get mad. We drove for about twenty minutes before I said, *David, where are we going?* And he said, *We're going back to our car. I left the bong in it.* And that's what we did. We found our car and Hastings got the pipe and then we turned around and drove back to town.'

I was laughing, it was funny, and Elsbeth chuckled reluctantly. 'You see what I mean, though,' she said. 'They do whatever they like. Hastings needs a car, he borrows one from a car-yard. Flynn wants a pair of boots, he takes them out of a window display. They never think twice. I don't think they're *normal* – '

'What happened about the car? What happened when you got back to town?'

She laughed again, waving the tissue in her hand. 'Man, the guy at the car-yard was almost having a breakdown. He was so happy to finally see us, he gave us cups of coffee and cigarettes. David said he liked the car but he had to think about it. We put the bong in my handbag and went back to the motel and got stoned all afternoon.'

'That's a great story.'

'That's not the end of it, though. Hastings must have thought about the car a bit more. He rang Sasha and asked him to put three thousand dollars in his bank account on the Monday morning. On Monday we both phoned in sick for work and that afternoon David goes to the car-yard and tells the guy he's decided to buy the yellow car after all. *We've got a Mazda parked on the side of the road about thirty clicks from here,* he says, and tells this guy about our car. He doesn't mention that the engine is utterly cactus. *How much will you trade for it?* The guy was useless, he didn't know what to say. But that's what we did, in the end, traded the Mazda for the yellow car and paid the difference with the three thousand that Sasha had put into the bank. We drove home in a completely different car from the one we arrived in.'

'This was before you got the four-wheel drive, then.'

'Yeah, this was before the truck. We only had the yellow car for about a year. It was crappy. But the saddest thing was, the guy from the car-yard sent us Christmas cards for the next two years. Even when the yellow car was the size of a Coke can we got a Christmas card from the car-yard guy. We must have been his only customers for years. Probably for ever.'

Elsbeth nodded nostalgically. Her long lacquered nails had shredded the tissue to particles. 'I loved that car,' she sighed. 'I really loved the yellow car. It broke down all the time, but it had good memories. You know? It was such a good weekend.'

I looked away from her. We watched Jemima romping on the lawn, tossing the ball and chasing it round. Elsbeth smiled. 'She's cute, isn't she.'

'Yeah.'

'Sasha really loves her. He spoils her.'

'Hmm.'

'Hitler loved his dog too,' she said, melodrama claiming her again, at last.

Andy and I went to see Hastings in the hospital. Hastings was looking pale and bored. His left forearm was neatly bandaged white. We brought him chocolates and he seemed pleased to see us, but Elsbeth and Mrs Hastings did not, so we left, went back to Andy's place. We watched some TV with his housemates and then retired to bed.

I'd become a sex maniac since dispensing with my virginity and had told Andy I spent ninety-five percent of my time thinking about sex and the other five percent puzzling why I was always thinking about sex, but this night I wasn't in the mood. He accepted this, was even possibly grateful. We lay side by side beneath the covers, Andy tickling my chest while I stared at the ceiling. A small voice inside me wondered what else, who else, his hands had touched that day.

'Andy,' I asked, 'what are you going to do with your life?'

'I don't know. Fritter it away.'

'You're already doing that,' I said, unnecessarily. He laughed, though. He was not the sort of person who traded insults.

'Andy,' I said, 'you wouldn't ever hurt me, would you?'

'Break your heart, you mean?'

'Break any bit of me,' I said.

His fingers paused on my stomach and he lifted his head. In the moonlight that dodged the venetian blind I saw his grey eyes narrow on me, his fair hair flop as he sat up on an elbow. 'What makes you ask a question like that?' he said, and I could see he was deeply hurt, appalled.

Of all of them, Andy is the one who is now most hazy in my memory. I haven't forgotten him, I never will, but sometimes I wonder if I would recognise him, if I passed him on the street.

Sasha was cross with his friends in the days that followed the break-in at the factory; cross with Flynn, who hadn't been there, and cross with Andy, who had. He was blunt and sarcastic when he spoke to them and they, bewildered but knowing what was good for them, scuttled to the periphery and tried to make amends from a distance. He was brutal to the wounded Hastings, who took the fortnight off work and chose to spend most of that time at the bungalow, getting in Sasha's way. Sometimes Hastings would bring his dog Chopper with him, and the nuggety boisterous animal harassed Jemima to distraction. Hastings worked at a foundry, where he stood and sweated in searing temperatures, feeding coiled metal into a machine that cooked the coiling out, and he would often ponder aloud the misery of the wretch who'd landed the task in his absence. Sasha's dark eyes grew murderous: he put a deck-chair on the veranda and invited Hastings to sit in it, to stay in it, and to take his unruly canine with him. Hastings and Chopper lounged there day after day, Hastings nursing his slashed and sutured arm, smoking cigarettes and eating chips and letting Chopper chew the empty packets of each, and all the while Sasha grew furious and more furious.

'What's the problem, Sasha?' I asked one day, as he flicked peevishly through the stations and finally threw the remote-control at the television. The two of us were alone. It was the first time we had been alone since the night I originally met him, in the Greyhound's beer garden. I'd been nervous then, and I was more nervous now: I thought we'd become friends that night, but I was wrong. To him, I was just another presence in his house. Conversations between us rarely lasted more than minutes, and his typical approach to my existence was to overlook it. I was vaguely scared of him, and I admired him wildly.

'There's nothing on TV.'

I scooped up the remote and turned the television off. He went to the window and looked out. At the sight of Chopper, who was lunging at the punching-bag that hung on a chain from the bungalow's veranda and dropping like a stone after each attempt, he remarked, 'Idiot.'

I did not want him to be angry: I did not want to be alone with an irritable Sasha Johns, but more than that I wanted him to find my company pleasing. 'You've been in a bad mood since Hastings got hurt,' I said. 'What's wrong?'

'Everything's wrong.'

'Did something happen at that factory – something besides Hastings?'

'No.'

'What, then?'

For a minute he didn't answer and I wondered if I should just shut up. Then he said, 'Aren't I allowed to be in a bad mood occasionally?'

'Your friends don't like it. It bothers them.'

'I don't care. I'm sick of them. I'm sick of everything.'

'But what would you do, if you didn't do this?'

'Go on a holiday. I never get a holiday.'

'They know that they're in trouble, but they don't know why – '

'They know, absolutely.'

He swung away from the window and stalked around the living-room. He'd let his hair grow longer over winter and the chestnut hooks of it were like sickles at his throat. He was quite tall, and built strong; the bungalow sometimes seemed cramped, for him. He slumped against the table where he often sat with Flynn, drawing rough maps of buildings and inspecting recent hauls. 'I'm tired of thinking for them,' he sighed. 'I'm tired of battling incompetence.'

'It was an accident, not incompetence. You're a *criminal*, Sasha, you can't always expect things to go your way. Haven't you ever had an accident?'

He looked up, glowering. 'Not when it's inconvenient to have one, no,' he said. 'Not when it puts a job in jeopardy and ourselves at risk . . . It wasn't just Hastings, though. Flynn should have been there, he was supposed to be there. And he phones me at the last minute to say his car won't start, for God's sake, we'll have to go without him. I've told him, time and again, to make sure things like that don't happen. There's no excuse for that sort of crap. So we have to take Andy instead and he doesn't know what's going on, he's missed out on all the background and all the planning, I have to tell him what to do and where to go, all of which distracts me from what I have to do, and on top of that there's that imbecile Hastings who has to go sit in the truck and bleed all over it – '

He stopped, as if physically unable to continue, and laughed miserably. 'We looked like a gang of amateurs, Louie. It was bloody farcical.'

'Is that your problem – you looked silly? Those two guys who were with you that day, those strangers – were you hoping to impress them?'

Sasha folded his arms and gave me a long look and refused to answer, and it made me giggle. 'Old pride took a bit of a battering, did it?'

'Be quiet.'

'No, no, I have to know – did you fall very far down the criminals' hierarchy? All the way to the bottom?'

Sasha closed his eyes and shook his head, pained.

'Because if you did, you know, I'll start looking for some new friends.'

'I am no longer talking to you,' he said shortly. 'Please don't talk to me.'

'What a delicate business this is – I never realised it before. I thought you were dumb beasts, acting on your instincts, but you're actually very sensitive, aren't you?'

'Why don't you go home?' he asked. 'I'm sure I hear your mother calling you.'

We smiled at each other, and neither of us moved, and in the stillness and the silence we heard Chopper hit the ground again. Sasha ran a hand through his hair and went to the sink, where he filled a glass with water and drank it all. We'd stopped laughing now.

'Andy will be back soon,' I said; he'd taken Hastings to the hospital for a check-up. 'I'll leave then.'

'With a bit of luck they'll overdose that useless bastard,' Sasha replied.

'You like Hastings,' I told him, 'remember? Sasha, if you keep this up, if you keep punishing them, they'll leave you. Everything you've created – your business, its connections – will be wasted, and for what? Things didn't go perfectly. Sometimes things won't, no matter how careful you are. They know they botched it, you've ground it in their faces. Now you've got to cheer them up. Bring them back together now, before it gets worse. Andy and Flynn and Hastings aren't business acquaintances, they're your *friends*. But without them you'll have no business and no friends.'

Sasha pondered this. 'They wouldn't leave,' he decided. 'They've got nowhere to go.'

'I reckon you're wrong.'

He looked down at the glass he still held in his hand. '*Cheer them up*,' he drawled. 'They're not children, Louie.'

'You all behave like you are, most of the time. You're a spoilt brat. You're an arrogant, spoilt brat.'

He eyed me coolly: for a moment I thought he was going to throw a tantrum, but he spoke instead. He said, 'I want an ice-cream.'

As we walked to the milkbar he said, 'My mother is having a birthday party in a couple of weeks. She's going to be fifty. We're having a barbecue in the garden because of it. You can come, if you like.'

'Just me?' I asked. I had Jemima on a leash, she was pulling my arm out of its socket. I suddenly wanted him to say *yes*, just me.

'You'd be a bit bored, wouldn't you, if it were just you? You'd better bring your beau. Flynn will be there too, because my mother feels sorry for him.'

'Oh.'

'I'll trust you to make sure Andy brushes his hair and wears something without holes. Please don't bring anything to eat or drink, it will be catered.'

'I'll make a cake anyway.'

'How sweet and talented of you. I'm sure it would be delicious but no, thank you all the same. Your presence alone will be enough: expect an invitation in the mail.'

And, sure enough, three or four days later the invitation arrived, with raised grey lettering on creamy, scented paper. I wore a dress to that party. I didn't wear it for Mr and Mrs Johns's hospitality, or for Andy's sake, but for Sasha. He had never seen me wearing a dress.

It was held in November on a warm, clear day, and there were eighty or ninety guests in the vast rear garden, milling at the barbecue and twitching fingers in the pool. The hosts had hired, or perhaps actually owned, a huge marquee, and tables of food and glasses were set out in its shade. People were eating prawns off hand-painted plates and dabbing their mouths with ivory-coloured linen. Women in heels were sinking spikes into the lawn. There were glittering streamers festooned amongst the trees, there was a banner printed with the words *Happy 50th Birthday Jennifer* flapping against the house, there was a stereo with speakers perched in the branches, and there was a bartender in tails behind a portable bar. 'It's like Gatsby,' I marvelled, and Andy said, 'I bet Sasha's wearing white.'

He wasn't. He was talking with a group of avuncular-looking gentlemen. 'Hello,' he said, over his shoulder. 'Thank you for coming. Get yourselves a drink.'

We did. The glasses had golden lengths of ribbon wound around their stems and the bartender mixed cocktails in a silver shaker. 'It's wonderful,' I breathed. 'Everything looks wonderful.'

Andy said, 'It's a tacky, blatant display of wealth.'

'That sounds like something Sasha would say.'

'I bet he hasn't, though.'

'Don't you like having a rich friend? I do.'

'What's good about it?' Andy asked tartly. 'He's never had a miserable day in his life.'

He was still pissed off about Sasha being angry at him. 'Go home,' I scolded, 'if you're going to be grumpy all afternoon.'

But he stayed, and he brightened up. I didn't know anyone and he pointed out the people he recognised, cousins and aunts and grandparents. 'That's his sister,' he said. 'Sasha's sister, Alexandra, in the red jacket, with that tall guy. His mother is over there, blue dress, talking to that fat lady. That's his father at the barbecue. The dentist man.' We shuddered.

'There's Jemima, look. They've put a bow around her neck. Come here, girl.'

She didn't, we had no food. We grabbed a table and the chairs had golden balloons tied to them, hovering on golden threads. The music stopped while the machine shuffled the discs, the conversation felt no lull. I gazed everywhere, remembering how I'd thought parties like this never happened, not in real life. Andy fetched a plate of chicken wings and herb bread and a waiter came by and offered us champagne.

Sasha strolled over to our table. 'Thanks for coming,' he said again, and dabbed a finger in the puddle of chicken marinade. He licked it clean while he scanned the crowd over our heads. 'What did you get for your mother?' I asked.

Sasha smiled at someone beyond us, glanced down distractedly. 'Sorry?'

'What did you get your mother for her birthday?'

'Something. A bracelet thing. I gotta go. Are you bored?'

'We might be,' Andy sighed, but Sasha was vanishing. He dodged the guests to reach the one he'd smiled for, an exotic lean girl with black hair falling like satin around her shoulders, a girl who looked as though a lot of money had been spent on her. I smoothed my dress over my knees. It wasn't really a pretty dress, I decided. I'd had it for a few years and it was tired, I should probably throw it away.

'We don't have to stay long,' I said.

Andy nodded. 'But let's drink a heap of cocktails first,' he said.

We grinned conspiratorially and I remembered that, once, I had craved Andy's attention, had almost swooned when I finally got it. There had been a time when I'd dreamed about him day and night, when a glimpse of him would stop me in my tracks, when I could have killed to have that wonky smile appear for me and hear that smoke-ruffled voice say my name. But I was not that girl any more, and I had begun to long for other things. Now I reached for his hand.

'Nah,' I said. 'Let's go home.'

We stood, and Mrs Johns said, 'Where are you going? You're not leaving, are you? I was coming over to talk to you.'

We looked stricken at each other, and I sank down. Andy offered her his chair and went to get himself another. Closer, I saw her face was lined and her hair had the false sleekness of a recent, professional dye. She was also extremely tipsy and a lipstick-smudged champagne glass was swaying in her hand. I thanked her for inviting us and wished her a happy birthday, to which she replied, 'Keep your congratulations to yourself. And don't call me Mrs Johns. My name is Jennifer. I've seen you before, haven't I? You're one of Sashy's secret friends.'

'I'm Louie,' I said. 'I'm not a secret.'

'Louie. *Secretive*, I meant. Sasha has many, many secretive friends.

He's very popular, my kid. That's good, isn't it? Imagine a child with no friends, how poignant.'

'I don't mean to be secretive. My mother would be cross if she thought I was being that.'

'Would she?' Jennifer looked surprised. 'I think it's rather funny. All these important, serious little people running around the back garden. Zooming about in their little cars.'

I smiled stickily; Jennifer slurped from her glass and rattled on.

'When Sashy was a boy he had a lovely cubby-house, a great fancy thing his father bought for him, and his friends would visit and spend hours playing in it. And that's what you all remind me of, kids playing in a cubby-house. You're a bit bigger now, and the cubby-house is rather fancier, but you're still kids, still playing. Like puppies.'

A splash of champagne leapt the rim of her glass and soaked through the tablecloth. Andy returned with a chair and sat down. 'Why do you come here, Andrew?' Mrs Johns inquired. 'To play in the cubby-house?'

Andy blinked. 'The bungalow,' I prompted.

'A bungalow!' Jennifer squawked, her attention pouncing heavily back to me. 'Wash your mouth with soap, young lady! That – *thing* – over there, for the hideously expensive construction of which I sacrificed a huge chunk of my beautiful garden, is a fully operational *granny flat*. Bungalow my butt. Sasha can call it a bungalow if he wants to but we all know it's a granny flat and it's supposed to contain a *granny*.'

I chuckled but Jennifer Johns had become suddenly reflective, and stared pensively into her glass. 'We built it for my mother-in-law,' she said. 'The poor old darling was demented. Deaf, not altogether cluey any more. You know how they get, I'll get like that myself one day, my children say I already am. But she died before we got the roof tiled. Quietly felled by a nocturnal stroke.'

'That's a shame,' I said. Andy remained mute. Mrs Johns squinted at me.

'A shame?' she rasped. 'Are you joking?'

I nodded, then shook my head hopelessly, but Jennifer was staring malevolently at the bungalow. 'I can't stand the vile thing,' she said. 'Every time I see it I think of my poor garden, ravaged and decimated. I wanted to turn it into a glasshouse but then we had a better idea and flung Sashy out into it.'

'He likes it.'

'Yes,' she replied. 'It keeps him close. I would worry about him, if he packed his bags and lived elsewhere. It's terrible having children: don't ever do it, Louie.'

I thought she was about to treat us to a gory and long-winded description of childbirth but she said, 'Children are grief. Grief. You never have a single moment free of worry from the minute they arrive. You spend your life wondering how they are, what they're getting into, where their lives are going, expecting at any moment that dreadful knock at the door, *Mrs Johns, do you have a son* . . . And they don't care. Children laugh at the fear they cause. Perhaps this is nature's way, I don't know. My kids call me a hag, but I've tried to be a good mother. I want them to be happy. I've never pressured them to do anything they haven't wanted to do. I haven't forced them one way or the other. I have given them freedom, I hope. When I was a young woman I was told you were nothing without a career but you were also nothing without a husband and kids. I got both, because I would have been a failure otherwise, but I feel I've failed anyway. I have everything – lovely possessions, a nice husband, beautiful children – but I haven't lived the life I hoped I would. Maybe nobody does, but I'm giving my children the chance. Do what you like, I tell them. Don't ask me for advice, for I've no right to give you any. Depend on no one. Stand on your own two feet and do whatever you like. And they do. Alexandra is an artist. She got that talent from me, but I wasted mine, let it die, studied formulas and chemical tables instead. There's a certain artistry in them, I suppose. As for Sashy, well, he drifts. He won't work, won't study. I worry about him, but I secretly respect him. He lives so completely on his own terms, he's utterly unhampered by expectations. Look at him – he has his eye on that girl. Katie. Alexandra's friend. She's a chef, you know.'

I sought Sasha through the crowd, found him deep in conversation with the exotic chef. He was propped against a tree trunk, wearing clothes I'd never seen before. He scuffed the grass, flourished a hand, shook back his glossy hair – a performance I'd never seen before, which gave me a stab of envy.

Jennifer Johns was raving on, her tone relentlessly forlorn. She had taken Andy's hand and was peering into his eyes. 'I thought

Sashy would die,' she was saying. 'For years I expected him to die at any moment. I don't know why, there was nothing wrong with him. He was never ill. He just seemed too lovely to survive. I'd look at him and understand that he was simply not long for this world. When he became a teenager and started to grow I thought, Oh, don't grow, you're growing into your grave. Don't become so handsome, you're breaking my heart, you'll be such a darling corpse. Is that a strange thing to think, Andrew? Did your mother think those things?'

Andy's eyes skimmed the tabletop nervously. 'I don't know, Mrs Johns.'

'She wouldn't tell you if she did. A mother can't tell her child she expected him to drop dead at any moment. I don't feel it so much any more, I don't know why. Maybe it's because his life is very much his own now. He's twenty-three, not a child. He's no longer mine to lose.'

'For God's sake, Mum, shut up.'

Jennifer Johns straightened and stared blearily at her daughter. 'My other baby,' she told us huskily. 'The scary one. I never worried about *her* dying, she's as tough as a bullock. Alex, have you met Louie? Sashy's new friend.'

Alexandra's severe expression did not change. 'You're being a bore, Mum.'

'Poor mother. Every time I open my mouth I'm boring.'

'You're showing off. You always show off when you're drunk.'

'Drunk! I'm a long way from being drunk.'

'Just *go away*,' Alexandra snarled. 'Sasha's friends don't care what you have to say. Go and bore someone else. Go and bore Dad. He married you.'

Jennifer's lashes fluttered and she looked fretfully at us. 'Did I bore you?' she asked. 'I apologise, awfully.'

'You didn't – '

'Louie says I didn't, see?'

Alexandra would not be moved, and Jennifer rose majestically with her glass. 'That's what happens,' she said, sadly stoical. 'You raise them and worry about them and they say you're a sodden nuisance. Which I am, but aren't I allowed to be? It's my birthday. Never have children, Louie. You have been warned.'

She lifted her head and moved, wonkily, off. I was glad to see her go: there was a feeling of malady and uselessness that wafted from her. Alexandra smiled at us. 'I'm sorry,' she said. 'How are you, Andy? How were your exams?'

'Have you met Louie, Alex?'

I'd seen her from a distance, but I'd never spoken to her before. She did not seem to spend much of her time at the house. She was tall, like her mother, and rather pretty, with the Johns dark skin and chestnut curls. She looked from Andy to me and back again. 'You two aren't – going out together, are you?' she asked. 'Andy, you never told me! Well, congratulations. You look really cute together.'

Andy and I exchanged a sheepish look. He knew – I think he knew it better than I did – that our relationship was unravelling: not because we didn't like each other, but because we didn't like each other enough. It was subsiding like a wave or a season, in a natural, painless kind of way. Still, it was nice to know we looked the part. Alexandra sat down and picked up a chicken wing. 'It's rude of Sasha,' she said, 'to leave you here alone.'

'He's got his own interests,' Andy observed. Alexandra smirked around the chicken bone.

'Hasn't he. Many and varied. Mum,' she said, 'pretends not to know what goes on in the bungalow. She pretends Sasha's fleeting visitors are great friends in a great hurry. She knows very well he's selling drugs in there. One day you guys will make a mistake and then she'll discover all the other stuff that goes on, as well.'

'I think you're confusing us with other people,' Andy replied, but I saw that she knew everything and wanted us to know that she knew. The jewellery she wore had been given to her by her brother. He'd talked to her about his schemes. He had defended her against unwanted male attentions and she had seen the scraped knuckles he occasionally brought home. Sasha and Alexandra, I guessed, stayed up late sharing cigarettes and stories. Probably there were things he reserved for her consideration only, things none of his friends would ever know: hers was a special place in his affections, one that we would never equal or invade. The alcohol and the sunshine were making me affectionate and I thought about my own little brother and sister, whom I often struggled to tolerate, and I resolved to be kinder to them.

Andy and Alexandra were talking about pottery. I knew she was an artist and I looked at the plates and bowls scattered around. 'Did you make these?' I asked her. 'They're beautiful.'

She shrugged and thanked me. 'Is this what you do for a living?' I asked. 'Pottery? How wonderful.'

'Show Louie your studio,' said Sasha. He was alone and, glancing around, I could not see the cook. He sat down and looked at me. 'It's very interesting,' he added.

'I'm sure she doesn't want to see it – '

She was right, I didn't want to, but I prised open my mouth and said, 'I'd love to.'

We left Andy and Sasha sitting there, and as I trailed after her I ached to know what the two of them would talk about, what I was going to miss.

She led me through the great house and that was the first time I had been inside it, it had never occurred to Sasha to show me around. When Alexandra realised this she took me on a tour and I saw rooms that were lived in and rooms that weren't, rooms strewn with preparations for the party and rooms where the carpet was never called upon to cushion a heel. I thought you could get lost in such a house and they'd never trace the source of your screams. Alexandra's studio was in a loft above the garage and from its window I could see the party below. The guests had descended into seats, most of them, and the muffled sound of their laughter drifted up to me. I spotted Jennifer, clinking glasses with a tottering friend, and Jemima, sniffing surreptitiously at a plate. Alexandra waved a hand around and said, 'Well, here we are.'

It was stuffy in the studio, the air felt thick to breathe. The room smelt heavily of clay and paint and glaze. I thought of Flynn's muggy, steaming growing-room and suddenly wanted to be there, with Flynn, safe and away from here. My thoughts were skittering, I'd drunk too much and eaten almost nothing, and I shook my head clear.

There were plates and bowls arranged on a long table, some painted, some not. There was a potter's wheel in one corner, a refrigerator in another, a jar of flowers on the windowsill and a rug on the floor crunchy with gobs of clay. Every surface was streaked or lumpy with clay. Nothing was as interesting as Sasha made it out to be. 'How long have you been a potter?' I asked.

'I've always liked art. I discovered pottery when I was about sixteen.'

'Uh ha.' My boredom felt like it was seeping through my skin and I grappled to force it back in. 'So you make things on the wheel and then bake them in the kiln, is that right?'

'Then I paint and glaze them.'

'I don't know anything about art,' I confessed.

'I wish I knew more about other things,' Alexandra said. She'd perched on the edge of a wicker chair and she looked wistfully around the room. 'I wish I had never been interested in it and loved – I don't know – accounting, instead.'

'What? Why?'

She chewed her lip for a moment; then the words came out in a rush. 'I just wish I'd loved something nice and normal that would make me money and keep me happy and be – *real*,' she said. 'Art just doesn't seem real enough, not to get a person through life.'

'But look at these things you make!' I protested: I knew enough about art to know it was not to be slandered. 'You're an artist, Alexandra. You make things that will be here when you're not, things of beauty, things that give other people pleasure. The world's got enough accountants – you can't really want to be an accountant – '

'I don't,' she conceded listlessly. 'I just wish I had wanted to be something else.'

For a second we said nothing; then, 'At least you want to be *something*,' I told her. 'I don't want to be anything.'

She flicked up an eyebrow, just like her brother would. 'Oh, nothing?'

'Nope,' I said, 'nothing. Nothing.' The bleakness of it suddenly captured me: I wanted to be *nothing*. I wanted to be indispensable, I wanted to be liked. I wanted to be welcomed and missed. I pouted, and picked at a stray blob of clay. 'Nothing I can think of.'

'How old are you?'

'Nineteen.'

'A baby.' She laughed, unconvincingly. 'You've got time to find something you want to do.'

'. . . I haven't, though. Not very much time.'

'No,' she admitted, 'probably not. No one gets to be young for long any more.'

We looked at each other; I thought, again, of Flynn, sitting in his garage on a wonky stool, sitting on the kitchen floor waiting for his father to bring home a dog. I felt depressed enough to cry, and let my gaze slide away. Life is sad in strange ways: I could not see why this wealthy and discontented girl reminded me of a lonely, hopeful boy.

'I think you're a good artist,' I said. 'It would be a crime if you didn't do this thing you can do.'

Alexandra Johns smiled. She stepped from the chair, pushed up her sleeves and opened the iron hatch of the kiln. She reached in and drew out a small, nut-brown bowl. 'Here,' she said, 'I made it this morning. Please let me give it to you.'

She offered it to me and I stared at her slim, bare, bruised arms. The bruises told a story: someone had gripped her, and their grip was painfully tight. She saw me staring and then her injury caught her eye. 'Oh,' she said softly, 'look.'

'Who did that to you?' I asked. 'Alexandra?'

'. . . I don't know,' she murmured. 'I don't know how that happened.'

I hesitated, unsure what to say. Her cheeks had flushed bright red, and when she spoke her voice had the slightest tremor. 'Please take the bowl,' she said.

Immediately her hands were empty she whipped down her sleeves and spun back to the kiln, fastening the hatch and whisking away some dust. Brusque now, she said, 'If you want it painted, bring it over in a few weeks and I'll do it for you. I'll be a bit busy until Christmas but I could do it after that, it won't take long.'

'I like it just as it is.'

'Well,' she said, 'it's up to you.'

I looked at the bowl, dredging for words. 'Thanks, Alex. If there's ever anything I can do – '

'Come on,' she said, shunting me towards the door, never looking me in the eye. 'We'd better go outside, Mum will be giving her speech in a minute.'

Andy and Sasha were deep in hushed conversation with Flynn, who had finally arrived. He didn't look anything like the way I'd just been picturing him – he didn't look like a lonely, hopeful boy. He looked like his usual self, and he had taken my chair. They gave me only a fleeting glance. 'Who's going?' Andy asked.

'Just the four of us.'

'Why three o'clock?'

'Oh, you know. It's a nondescript hour. The neighbours might be out.'

Flynn plucked the cigarette from his mouth and said, 'I think morning would be better. It's the sort of thing you would do in the morning.'

'Yeah, I see your point.' Sasha looked at me. 'You got a bowl,' he said.

'What are you talking about?'

'Remember how you were saying we needed cheering up? Well, something's come along to cheer us up. If you were going to help a friend move out of his house, what time would you start?'

'In the morning, I suppose.' It was the first time he had asked my opinion on anything concerning the business. 'Why waste half the day?'

Sasha blew smoke at the ceiling of the marquee. 'OK,' he said finally. 'Ten o'clock.'

Flynn nodded, satisfied. 'What day?' I asked.

'Never you mind. You're not invited.'

'But it was my idea!' I squeaked. 'Please, Sasha. I hate getting left behind all the time. I've never caused a problem, I've never stuffed up, but I never get to do anything fun. Please? Anyway, it would look good to have a girl with you. No one suspects a girl. It's the sort of thing a girl would do, too, help her friend move house.'

Flynn looked dubious. 'It'll be scary,' he said. 'You'd be scared.'

'I wouldn't. Please, Sasha. Please?'

Sasha and Andy glanced at each other. 'It's up to you,' Sasha told him. 'Your responsibility.'

Andy looked at me and I looked back with every shred of affection I'd ever felt for him. 'Only if you promise,' he said, 'to stay out of the way and do what you're told.'

'Thank you!' I yipped: I would have kissed him with gratitude, but that would have been embarrassing.

'All right, then,' said Sasha. 'Next Sunday, ten o'clock, decoy in tow.'

Flynn said, 'Louie, you're wearing a dress.'

Alexandra sits with her head bowed. We can hear her parents talking in the garden. They don't know that we're here. They're asking each other where Sasha is. Sasha is in the loft with us, but he doesn't move. He has hardly moved all afternoon. Jemima, bundled up and sleeping on his feet, has moved more often than he has.

Alex says, 'I started to think I deserved it.'

Sasha moves; he looks at her; I know what he's like inside, like a tiger on a chain. Alex sees that everyone's watching her and she says, 'Well, I did, didn't I? I'm supposed to be smart. I'm not meant to let a man hit me. I'm not meant to give him money and forgive him and tell him that I love him. I know that, but I did it anyway. And it made me look stupid.'

She leans forward, her palms turned up to us. 'Don't you see?' she pleads. 'After a while, I didn't *want* to tell anyone what was happening. Because it made me look stupid.'

Sasha says, 'Give me a cigarette, Flynn.' So I chuck him the pack.

'That was your mistake,' Kate says to Alex. 'You stopped talking. One minute you wouldn't shut up about Daniel, and then you wouldn't say a word. That's when I started to wonder what was going on. Remember, Sasha, I mentioned it to you at your mother's party. That Alex had gone quiet and odd. And you'd noticed it already.'

Alexandra says, 'Do you remember when I went to the loft with Louie that day, Mum's birthday?'

I look at Sasha, who says, 'What about it?'

'She saw bruises on my arms. It made me want to stuff her head in the kiln. I was so embarrassed, you know? I was so ashamed.'

She's honestly surprised to see the bruises on her arm, the dark smudged shadows of Daniel's grip. She can't decide when she must have got them. He is always grabbing her arm, sometimes in a friendly manner. His grasp is always a fraction too tight. It pinches and hurts her, and once when she protests he says, 'That's not a pinch – this is.' And the crescents his nails left in her flesh had blazed, a pair of them grinning in her skin.

It always happens when she least expects it and it puzzles her why she can't fathom some predictability to it. Afterwards he explains where she's gone wrong and she sees it then, but as hard as she tries she can never see it coming, can never sidestep or go silent in time. It doesn't always end in a welt:

sometimes the hurt isn't easily seen or explained. Once she challenges him to a race on the video speedway and when she wins she hoots with laughter, and, 'If you think that's an achievement,' he says, 'to win a ridiculous video game, you're a very pathetic person.' Walking down an empty street late one frostbitten night she tells him that she sometimes imagines herself as the last person alive, the sole occupant of the world. 'Yeah,' he sneers, 'you would. You'd wish death on everyone.'

He seems to have an excess of hatred. She notices that his conversation often begins with the words, 'Don't you hate . . .' And sometimes it's something she doesn't hate at all. She finds it easy to agree, anyway. She'll disagree only when she has the energy. If he loses an argument he'll sulk, or claim she wore him down – or he might concede she's right after all, that she's managed to change his mind.

Or a plate might go flying. Or he'll swing his arm dramatically and pretend he doesn't know what she's worried about when she flinches away. Once he clamps a hand over her mouth to quieten her and she struggles until she sweats to break herself free, to get a gasp of air.

One night she wakes to find him raging round the bedroom, whipped into a fury because he is cold. He stomps in the darkness and kicks the cupboard and walls; when she offers him the blankets he tears them from her, leaving her goose-bumped and naked. One night, a dinner he cooks doesn't work out as planned: he slams the saucepans on the kitchen floor and food goes everywhere; he will not eat the pizza she buys instead.

All this frightens her, but what can she say? Which words will help her explain? *He pulls my hair, he is cold at night, we go out for drinks and he hardly says a word . . .* people would look at her strangely, if she said she found that frightening. Once, she irons his clothes for him: she folds them neatly and stacks them up. And then a pile of job knockbacks comes in the mail and he throws the clothes on the floor and kicks them around the room. So what can she say about that? That the sight of a man booting underwear had been, to her, terrifying?

She starts to look more closely at people on the street: she starts to think, *Are you loved? Do you like it?*

The trouble is, whenever he hurts or frightens her, he seems to have reason, a reason she understands. She has a habit of speaking before she thinks, of telling pointless stories, of making jokes in the midst of seriousness. She guesses that this would be infuriating to someone who takes everything so seriously. Under the weight of the cold peculiar looks he gives her, she starts to have suspicions about herself. Maybe she is dizzy, vapid. Maybe her conversation is fatuous, half-witted, and she'd be wiser to keep her mouth shut. Maybe she knows nothing about life and has no right to an opinion. After all, life has been sweet to her. She's never known a day of discomfort. She's never gone without. She's got a nice family, a sprawling house. People have, all her life, been willing to like her. Things have not been that way for Daniel. He impresses upon her that his life has not been easy. He has a Troubled Background. He hadn't made friends in twelve whole years at school. When he was finished with that, his father had invited him to join the family's printing business. Daniel had refused. He wouldn't spend his life wandering a factory floor, imperiously overseeing the labouring of others. His mother was a distant woman, never at home, always at work, concerned with money, unconcerned with him. She had supported her husband's efforts to trap him. He considers himself to have been always lonely.

He tells her this story: he's walking home late one night, he's about fifteen at the time, and finds a kitten in the gutter, almost steps on the thing. The animal is soaked and cold and starving but comes to him cautiously, darting and mewling. Daniel takes it home, feeds it and locks it in the bathroom for the night. When he wakes next morning he finds the creature leaping around the kitchen, his father angry and his mother pale-faced.

'My father wanted me to put it back where I'd found it,' Daniel explains. 'He decided I couldn't have it because I was unreliable, I wouldn't care for it, I'd let it become someone else's responsibility. He didn't even ask me if I would look after it, he just assumed I would not.'

'Did you take it back?'

'No. I hadn't found it anywhere. The road is nowhere. You can't leave an animal in a gutter.'

'So what happened?'

She expects him to say that the father promptly drowned the beast in a bucket and made Daniel watch.

'We ended up keeping it,' he shrugs. 'It became my mother's cat. Stripey. Dumb animal, doesn't know its head from its arse. Spoiled rotten. Sleeps on her bed.'

'Well.' Alexandra blinks, puzzling over what she's meant to say. She knows she has to take Daniel's side but what, exactly, is Daniel's side? What on earth is he protesting about? 'Well,' she says, 'it worked out for the cat, at least.'

'Only because my mother felt sorry for it. She never doted on me the way she dotes on that cat.'

'But you got what you wanted. The kitten got to stay.'

'Yeah, and my father tells everyone that it was him who saved its life.'

He left home as soon as he was able. He supervised at the factory until he'd saved enough to buy a car, which he drove across the desert to the other side of the continent, never to return. He got a job cleaning offices and sees himself, in the mirror, growing to look more and more like his father. His parents ring him every fortnight and he says he wishes they wouldn't. His younger sister and older brother phone him every month or so. He speaks of them fondly but doesn't ring them in return. He is an uncle several times over but has never seen his niece and nephews. Alexandra suggests he visit his family at Christmas and that is another mistake. He tells her it would lead to fights and hatred, can't she understand? He would have thought that was obvious.

He remembers his old girlfriends and often talks about them. He has a habit of comparing Alexandra with them. 'Justine used to tenderise steak with a mallet before she cooked it,' he will say. He claims not to have the slightest scrap of interest in Alexandra's past boyfriends but he is sullen when he discovers that one of them visits her for coffee. He claims to love fat women and draws her attention to those that catch his eye, but finds a ripple of cellulite on Alexandra's thigh to be utterly repulsive. He teases her about it in a playful tone but he won't touch it. She points out that he is considerably less muscular than she prefers her men to be and this, too, is a mistake. 'I can't help my build!' he cries. 'It's in my genes! But that – *that* – you should do exercise to get rid of that!'

Women have broken his heart. He falls hard and the feeling isn't always matched. One woman had an affair on the side the whole time she went out with him. Others promised the world and then snatched it back. He shifted house to be nearer to one woman, caught a plane to meet another at an airport. These were gestures of devotion, but the women reacted like he was a fanatic and a freak. He's wasted months and money and hope on women. He can't get out of his head how badly he's been treated. There are times, he tells her, when he believes he hates women, every last one of them. 'How can I trust you,' he asks her, 'when your breed is so treacherous? You want love, but if I love you, you leave. Even you were a tramp when I met you, sleeping with anyone you picked up. That's how this relationship will end: you'll return to your old ways.'

'No,' she says tiredly, with a sense that she'd rather die than meet or see or talk to a man ever again, 'my gallivanting days are over.'

'Why?' he asks. 'Because you've snagged yourself a lawyer?'

She doesn't love him, but she doesn't leave him. There's good in him; he worries about her. There's humour in him; he'll play and joke sometimes. If she can teach him not to hate himself, to stop dwelling on his errors and feeling so endlessly sorry for himself, he might always be like that. If she can learn to be more sensitive, quieter, more patient, he'll find no reason to be angry with her. If they can somehow balance each other out, they can go to the country. She wants to go so much. She's wanted to live in the country since she was a child. She can see it, smell it, but it isn't coming closer.

Every day the mailman brings rejection. Law firms all over the country are turning him down. They haven't the money or the work to support another lawyer. He will not throw these letters away: he preserves them in a folder. She hates them as much as he does. This, at least, is something they agree about.

Hastings arrived with Chopper, both of them yawning at half past nine. The four-wheel drive was spangling from a journey through a carwash. Hastings plonked his heavy frame in an armchair and asked, 'What's the story?'

'I went through the house last night,' Sasha told us. 'We'll have to park the truck on the front lawn but that shouldn't be a problem. There's a window at the back of the building that's shielded from the neighbours. Slats of glass, so bring the leather gloves. We don't want anyone getting *hurt*.'

Hastings rubbed his arm, now free of swaddling and stitches but bearing a nasty, puckered scar, and chose not to retaliate.

'The street is populated by oldies and young families. It's a nice morning so people might be wandering around. We'll do this as fast as we can but remember to be casual. We have, after all, been invited.'

And we had. The owner of the house, someone called Elliot, had sourced us through a trustworthy friend. He wanted us to relieve him of his television, video recorder and stereo system. It would look like he'd been robbed, but what had really happened was a business transaction. He would claim his losses on his insurance and the replacement equipment he'd get would be newer, bigger, brighter. We got to keep his old stuff.

'Do you do this type of job often?' I asked, for it seemed dangerous and the rewards paltry, when tricky Flynn could steal ten video machines a day.

'This isn't one of our most requested services, no,' Sasha replied. 'But it has its benefits. As robbers, we shan't be taking only those things our employer wishes to be rid of. We must uphold, after all, the reputation of robbers the world over. There's a brand-new bar fridge so Hastings, bring the trolley. There's a computer and a load of games. But what particularly caught my eye was a rather handsome Ramset gun.'

Hastings looked up alertly. 'A Ramset?'

'What's a Ramset gun?' I croaked.

'What sort of condition is it in?'

'It looked good, it was in its box and all.'

'What's this dude doing with a Ramset, anyway?' asked Flynn. He had his chair tilted backwards and his boots on the dining table. 'You need a licence for them, don't you?'

'He puts up the signs for houses for sale. He must use it for that.'

'Cool,' said Hastings.

'What is a Ramset gun?' I croaked again. Sasha turned to me.

'And,' he said, as if he'd never left the original topic, 'don't you think it's handy to know, for the future, the whereabouts of a house full of shiny new electrical goods, freshly replaced by the insurance company, as well as knowing how to safely access that house?'

I nodded my dumb agreement but the whole job seemed fraught with potential disaster and the talk of guns made my stomach skitter. I prayed they were as confident as they seemed. I prayed they were as clever as they considered themselves to be. I felt the warmth drain from my flesh when Andy handed me a pair of woollen gloves. 'What are these for?' I stammered.

'Put them on. Don't take them off until we're home again.'

'Surely they wouldn't dust for fingerprints, would they?'

'You never know.' He watched me tug on the gloves and said, 'Only an idiot doesn't wear gloves, Louie. Always, everywhere, gloves.'

I nodded glumly, and he looked me in the eye. 'You don't have to come, if you don't want to.'

'No, I want to,' I hastened. 'I trust you.'

'Good,' said Sasha. 'Let's go.'

It took us twenty minutes to drive to the house. On the floor of the truck were blankets and ropes and the trolley, which rattled over bumps. Hastings drove and Chopper and Sasha sat alongside him; Andy, Flynn and I were relegated to the back. They were in a relaxed, talkative mood and it seemed that only I scanned the traffic everywhere, eyes peeled for a police vehicle. My hands were sweating in the gloves and I clamped them under my knees.

The suburb was a sedate one and I saw what Sasha had cautioned we might see: people with the gall to be out on the streets, exercising dogs and wheeling prams. We pulled up outside a house and Sasha directed Hastings where to park the truck. I looked at the house and ran through everything I knew about its owner, where he worked, the hours he worked, the names of close friends and relatives who might drop unexpectedly by.

We left the truck sitting boldly on the front lawn, its hatch door hoisted innocently open and its radio on loud. We walked down the driveway to the rear of the house. There were trees here, and shade, and I lurked about in this protection while Flynn cut an obvious slash in the flyscreen and then removed the slats of glass that made up the window. Sasha gave him a boost and he wriggled through the gap he'd made. There was a minute of stillness before the back door opened and Flynn stood there smiling, cobwebs in his hair. 'If I knew you was coming,' he said, 'I'da baked a cake.'

Elliot's house was decorated like every other house occupied by a man without a sense of style: nothing quite complemented anything else, nothing was quite tasteful, objects of beauty were actually objects of dusty ugliness, but you could see the mind that was convinced otherwise. The others spread out and I wandered aimlessly from room to room. 'Grab whatever you like,' Hastings encouraged me, but I dared take nothing, appalled at the frailness of my criminal mind.

They took, first, the things they'd arranged to take, the television, the stereo, the video recorder. They carried these things to the four-wheel drive and stacked them inside. They left the door of the house standing open and Chopper ran in and out, bulldozing his way everywhere. Flynn raided the fridge, found a bag of popsicles and shared them around. They worked quickly, glancing to the clock, but calmly, taking time to change the radio station to something they preferred. Hastings disconnected the computer and he and Andy carted its various pieces to the truck. Flynn took the shampoo because he'd run out at home. Sasha swept compact discs into a pillowcase and, doing so, caught sight of me. 'Bored?' he asked.

'No – '

'Go to the bedroom,' he said. 'Look in the sock drawer.'

'What am I going to find in a sock drawer? Socks?'

'You'd be surprised what you find in a sock drawer,' he said.

I did as instructed and pawed amongst colourful sock balls. 'There's nothing!' I hollered, suspecting I was the victim of a criminal's joke. Andy passed the door, answering machine in hand, and winked at me. 'There's just socks in here, isn't there?' I asked him, but he'd gone.

'Are you squeezing them?' Sasha called from down the hall.

'What?'

'Are you squeezing – oh, for God's sake.' He marched into the bedroom, grabbed a pair of socks and crushed them in a fist. 'Nothing,' he said, and tossed them aside. He dug deeper, biting his lip. That close to me, I could smell the tangy aftershave he'd used. 'Hello,' he said, and drew out a flat blue booklet: a passport. He flipped through it, then tucked it into a pocket.

'What do you want that for?'

'Because we want everything. Keep squeezing those socks.'

He scanned the room, looking into the cupboard and under the bed. I scrunched the socks, feeling ridiculous, until a pair made a crunching sound in my hand.

'Oh!' I said. 'Bingo, I think.'

'Found it?'

'I think so.'

'How much?'

I unfurled the socks and counted the money that fell out of them. 'Five hundred.'

Sasha came over to look at it. 'Rent money,' he deduced. 'Ours now. See what I found.'

He held up a rigid green plastic dildo and buzzed it in my face. I scrambled backwards and was poised to shriek when the doorbell rang. We froze and stared at each other.

'I'll handle it – '

'No,' I said. 'Let me.'

Sasha hesitated, his dark eyes examining me. Then he said, 'Take your gloves off.'

I stripped them from my hands and stepped into the hall, vaguely aware of Flynn crouched in the shadows, of Hastings slipping away with the struggling Chopper in his arms. I saw a woman in the doorway and as I walked toward her I summoned the girl I used to be, the girl who knew nothing, who'd never done anything wrong. 'Hi,' I chirped.

'Hello,' the woman started, and I saw that she was disconcerted by the sight of me, a girl in clean clothes and ribbons, a kid. 'I was wondering – what's going on?'

I'd reached the front door, and looked at her quizically. She was middle-aged and looked like she would be friends with my mother. 'Going – ? Oh, Elliot's shifting out. He's putting up signs today but we said we didn't need him to be here. He helped my boyfriend and me shift last year so we're repaying the favour. Not what I'd prefer to be doing on a day like this, but anyway.'

I pulled the door and stepped out across the veranda, coaxing her away. She wandered to the truck and peered into its maw. I knew what she was seeing: electricity plugs and the smooth black surfaces of electrical equipment, their various switches and dials. 'We're taking the furniture tomorrow,' I blurted. 'Elliot's hiring a van.'

'He didn't tell me he was shifting out.'

'Oh,' I said, 'are you good friends with him? I love him. Don't you? I love his eyes. He's got the most gorgeous eyes, hasn't he?'

I hoped he had. Sasha hadn't been that specific. My heart was whacking against my ribs. I had a weird sense of being in the near vicinity of my body, but not actually in it; at the same time I felt sharper and more vital than I'd ever been, every cell within me sparking. The woman was looking at the truck and I was alarmed to think she was studying its number plate, composing a rhyme to recall it; I angled to distract her. 'El's mother is coming over this afternoon, to help,' I said. 'Do you know her?'

'No. I don't really know Elliot well. My husband and I like to keep a watch over the neighbourhood . . .'

I tried to seem confused, then 'Ah!' it dawned on me. 'That's good of you. My boyfriend and I got robbed a couple of months ago, we live in a block of flats and there's people around all the time, and not one single bastard – oh, sorry – I get so angry thinking about it. Not one single person bothered to ask what was happening. And they took everything. They took the necklace my mum gave me when I turned ten. I didn't care about losing the other things, you can replace them, but I want that necklace back, I really do. I cried, when they took that.'

I let my hands fall, having done what I could. If she'd asked me one more question then, I could not have answered it. Instead, she smiled sombrely at me. 'Yes,' she sighed, 'it's happened to us too.'

'It's cruel.'

'Yes.'

'People don't care about other people.'

'No.'

I blinked at her helplessly. She patted the truck's sea-green rump. 'Well,' she said, 'I'd best let you get back to it.'

'I don't mind,' I replied. 'I hate packing.'

'It's a terrible job.'

'Yeah. Well, thanks for coming over. I'll tell Elliot that you did. He'll be touched.'

The woman didn't seem very keen on that idea. 'Please don't,' she said. 'There's no need. People mistake concern for prying. I'd hate to look like the local busybody.'

I stood where I was for a minute or two, watching her walk away, before hurrying back to the house. The others had gathered in Elliot's bedroom and Flynn was peeping through the curtain. No one spoke until he shook his head and confirmed, 'She's gone. She's not coming back.'

'Let's go,' I whimpered. 'Let's get out of here.'

'Get that fridge on the trolley.'

'Sasha, forget it, we have to go now!'

He looked at me. 'Louie,' he sighed, 'you're doing my head in with your noise. The most suspicious thing we can do right now is run. Don't you think?'

That bruised me. 'Fine,' I said. 'You might like to know that she was memorising the number plate.'

'It doesn't matter . . .'

'The number plates are fakes,' Hastings told me. 'They don't belong to the truck.'

We carted the bar fridge to the four-wheel drive and were forced to linger stressful minutes more while Sasha sat on the veranda and blatantly smoked a cigarette. Hastings killed the time telling jokes. A man goes to the doctor to get the results of some tests. Doctor says, It's bad news, you've got cancer and you've got Alzheimer's Disease. The man says, Whew, thank goodness I haven't got cancer. 'Can we go now?' I begged.

'I think so,' said Sasha. 'Have we locked the front door?'

And then we were off and driving and the tension left me as we rolled along. I had one hundred dollars in my pocket and, soon, an idiot's grin on my face. No one had told me I'd done well, getting rid of the suspicious woman, but I didn't mind, I was pleased. They could discuss *ad infinitum* the job itself but they rarely singled out for praise someone who did something particularly heroic, as if doing so made lesser heroes of the rest of them. Flynn had complimented my canniness on the night we stole the tequila but I had been a stranger to them then, not part of the gang.

When we pulled unexpectedly into a laneway and Hastings cut the engine I felt a prickle of doubt and fear, but the others seemed unflustered and only Flynn jumped out of the truck. 'What's happening?' I whispered to Andy.

'Flynn's changing the number plates. Putting the real ones back on.'

'Why?'

'If that woman did decide to call the police,' he said, 'she'll have given them a description that we're not going to match.'

I was vaguely hurt, thinking perhaps they weren't as pleased with my work as I was myself, but Andy assured me, 'We do it every time we use the truck.'

'The truck,' mused Sasha, 'has a bit of an identity crisis,' and Hastings chuckled.

'What will Elliot say,' I asked, 'when he discovers you've taken more than you were supposed to take?'

'We,' Sasha reminded me. 'Not *you*, Louie – we.'

'What can he say? He's been robbed, hasn't he? The police might think it was a bit strange if someone got robbed and all that got taken was a cruddy television and a crappy stereo.'

I looked around at the cargo we carried, the snakepit of electrical cords at my ankles. 'But won't Elliot be mad?'

'Hopping, I guess.'

'He might dob you in.'

'He can't,' said Sasha. He hadn't turned in his seat; both he and Hastings had their eyes on the rear-view mirror, which reflected the road and anything that might come along it. 'Elliot silenced himself. That's what you get for being a gullible, dim-witted defrauder of insurance companies. You don't always lose only what you choose.'

'Maybe he'll pay you a visit, then,' I suggested. 'Come knocking at your door one night.'

'He was a weed,' said Sasha scornfully. I saw noses break, bones crack.

'We'd burn his house down,' Hastings told me. 'We'd burn his mother's house down.'

'We'd stuff a letterbox up his arse.'

'We'd fall about laughing.'

They laughed then and there, because they could. They were greatly cheered.

We left our stolen property in the truck, draped by a blanket, to be brought into the bungalow under cover of darkness and distributed from there. With a sunny afternoon to dispose of we got stoned and mucked around with the Ramset gun. A Ramset, I discovered, was a large metal nail-gun, and when you put an explosive charge in it and pulled the trigger it could drive a nail through brick, through concrete, through just about anything it liked. It made a tremendous bang when it did so and sent Chopper into a whirling frenzy every time. Flynn, Hastings and Andy seemed to think this thing delightful and slammed nail after nail into any hard surface they could find. I asked if I could have a go and the gun was heavier than it looked, and its long silver snout was thick and fierce. Hastings loaded it with the smallest charge and when I placed the muzzle of the gun against the fence and pulled the trigger, the kickback made me stagger. Hastings hooted, and I peered at my achievement. The flat head of the nail had been forced deep into the wood, leaving a cleanly gouged tunnel to mark its path. 'Cool, isn't it?' said Hastings.

'Sure,' I said doubtfully, 'great.'

Jemima didn't like the noise and she lay quivering on the decking, so I sat beside her and patted her and we watched from there. Elsbeth arrived and stood with us, saying nothing for a long time, her lip arched by what she saw. 'Sad bastards,' was her eventual response.

She knew the plans of the morning's expedition and asked how it had gone. 'I was the best,' I confided to her. 'I chased away the nosy neighbour and saved the day.'

The Handbrake was unimpressed. 'What do you want?' she asked. 'A medal?'

I shrank back, and she advanced. She said something strange. She said, 'Don't think anything good about Sasha. He doesn't think good about anyone else. Not even you.'

'She's jealous of you,' Sasha told me later, 'just like she's jealous of me. We're in the same besieged boat.'

It was night-time and I was sitting in one of the chairs outside the bungalow, drinking beer and looking at the stars. He had come to stand in the doorway and the light of the bungalow shone from behind him, filled with the explosions of computer games. He had a bottle and a glass in his hands.

'Hastings worships the ground you walk on. I can see how that would annoy her. She has nothing to be jealous of me about.'

'I'll tell you a story about Elsbeth,' he said. He stepped across the veranda and folded into the chair beside me, the light touching him where his bones met his skin. 'One night,' he began, 'Flynn, Hastings, Elsbeth and I left the Vicky Greene and started walking down the street. It was a nice night, like this one, and we'd been at the pub for quite a while. Hastings was walking ahead of the rest of us and, as he crossed the road, he walked between two cars that were parked against the gutter. He didn't touch the cars, he was just walking along, minding his business. But suddenly five guys jump out of one of the cars and start screaming that he's scratched the car as he went past. One of them must have whacked him with something because Hastings dropped like a rock, keeled over like he'd been shot. I don't think these guys had realised that Flynn and I were with him, and they were a bit surprised to see us, but they pretty much kicked the shit out of us anyway. At some stage while this is happening I looked around and saw Elsbeth, and she's sitting on the chest of this one guy, and he's flat on his back in the middle of the footpath, and she's got a handful of his hair and she's slamming his head up and down, up and down, bashing his brains out on the cement. She was screaming in his face as she did it, and every time she said a word she'd slam his head again. *Don't* – smash – *you* – smash – *dare* – smash – *hit* – smash – *my* – smash – *boy* – smash – *friend* – smash – *ever* – smash – *again* – smash smash smash – *do you hear me you stupid* – smash – *fucking* – smash – *wanker?* I'm telling you, it looked like there were going to be three dead guys out there: me, Flynn and that poor son of a bitch that Elsbeth was sitting on.'

I tilted my glass and drained the last few drops. 'So what happened?'

'Well, some guys we knew came out of the pub and saw what was going on; when they arrived, the guys who were kicking the crap out of Flynn and me split. They left their friend, there was nothing they could do for him. These friends of ours had to prise the Handbrake off that guy and she took a fistful of his hair with her. All this time Hastings is still out cold. A friend drove us home and Hastings came round in the car. He wouldn't believe that there had been a fight, but he wouldn't believe we'd been in the pub all night, either. He spewed on himself and slept for two days. And do you know what old Elsbeth had to say about the whole adventure?'

I looked at him through the darkness, and Sasha leaned closer to me. 'She usually keeps a Swiss army knife in her handbag,' he said, 'but for some reason she didn't have it with her that night. What she said was, *If I'd had my knife I would have killed that prick.*'

'She wouldn't have, though, would she?'

'You didn't see her.' He sat back, twisted the lid from the bottle and pitched the cap into the garden. He filled my glass and handed it back to me. 'As true as I sit here,' he said, 'I swear that she would have slit that man's throat if she'd had her knife.'

'Wow,' I said. Sasha nodded.

'That's why she will never tell anyone about what we do,' he said. 'That's why, no matter how much she hates me, she'll keep hanging around. We are her kind of people, and she knows it.'

We said nothing for a while; we sipped our beers and looked at the moon. The noise of the computer game was punctuated by the small, anxious screams of Flynn, as he battled to stay alive. I felt so happy to be sitting there, close to Sasha, with his friends at my back; at that moment, I would not have traded my position for a place amongst the stars.

'Louie,' he said eventually.

'Hmm?'

'I need you to do something for me. A favour. Is there a chance of you calling by here tomorrow?'

My gaze fell from the moon to him. 'Just me?'

'Just you.'

'. . . OK.'

I sank back in the chair, my arms around my knees, and smiled at the sky. I thought of the girls who had once made my life a misery, the snarky, giggling, imperious schoolgirls who had hitched up their dresses and spurned me as infinitely boring and uncool. What I would give to see them now, to still their prattle with my dangerous glance, to stalk past them in the company of my wolfish friends. They would be afraid to approach me, but from a distance they would seethe with envy and outrage. Those girls would glorify their school days as the best years of their lives but I knew now that I'd endured such purgatory for a reason: for revenge.

Sasha did not get straight to the point. He moved restlessly through the bungalow, making coffee, opening the windows, changing the music, tussling with his dog. I wondered how he had assured our privacy, what he'd said to Andy and the ever-present Flynn. Most likely he'd told the truth – *I want to talk to Louie, and I don't want you around* – and he'd have told them what he wanted to say, something I didn't know yet, something Sasha seemed oddly reluctant to disclose. I watched him sit down, stand up, tousle his hair with a hand. His nervousness was making me queasy. 'How's the chef?' I inquired.

'Who?'

'The girl you were talking to at the barbecue.'

'Kate? What about her?'

'Well, nothing,' I admitted. 'You just seemed interested in her the other day.'

'Well, she's an interesting woman. Would you like another coffee?'

I shook my head and his shoulders slumped. 'Where's all that junk from Elliot's place?' I asked, because it wasn't anywhere I could see.

His parents, no doubt, made unscheduled visits to the bungalow, and I was curious how he shielded his ill-gotten gains. 'You haven't sold it already, have you?'

He flicked a glance at the ceiling and my eyes went up.

'In the roof space?'

'Why waste it?'

I considered the smoke-stained ceiling and said, 'I'll be a bit cross if a bar fridge falls on my head.'

'No, that shouldn't happen. I had a carpenter reinforce it.'

'Ah.' Another valuable friend, the carpenter.

'. . . It's hot, isn't it,' he remarked. 'It's a hot day today.'

'I'm glad. We had a long winter. I like the heat.'

'Yeah, me too, I've nothing against it.'

'So why did you ask me to come here, Sasha?'

He did not resist being forced to the point. He sat down and looked intently at me over the cluttered plain of the coffee table. He said, 'You know my sister, Alexandra?'

'I've met her once.'

'Yes – she gave you a pot.'

I nodded; there was a packet of Flynn's forgotten cigarettes on the table and I shook one from the box. Sasha watched, evidently torn between frustration and relief at this distraction: he picked up some matches but he did not hand them to me, he simply dropped them closer.

'It's a nice pot,' I said.

'I'm worried about her.'

'Why?'

'I don't know,' he replied; he appeared perplexed by this insubstantial answer and scanned the floor around his ankles as if searching for words he'd dropped. He discovered, 'She has this boyfriend,' and lapsed once more into silence.

'. . . And?'

'And, something's not right. Something funny's going on. I don't know what it is and she hasn't said anything is wrong, but something is happening. I know it, but I can't explain it. You'll have to take my word.'

He said it all in a rush, as if impatient to be done. I dropped my match into the ashtray and looked at him, his face slightly reddened, his eyes cast down to watch his fingers pick agitatedly at a thread in the couch's seam. I realised, quite clearly, what he was talking about. I knew I could say, *Sasha, you're right,* and describe to him the bruises I had seen on his sister's arms. But, strangely, what I thought of was Flynn, and what Flynn's advice might be in this situation. Flynn would tell me to keep my information to myself for the time being, so I did. Flynn would tell me to abuse the position of power I unexpectedly found myself occupying, and I did.

For six months I had listened, responded, and learned, but beneath that spongy outer coating I had been carving a new person, a personality, with its own stance, its own will. I was no longer content to follow and appreciate: I wanted, now, to bully out a space of my own. I wanted them to value me; I wanted their respect. I sat forward.

'Why are you so ashamed of your concern for your sister, Sasha?'

He looked up quickly. 'I'm not.'

'You are. You're blushing.'

He reached for a smart retort, and lost heart. 'Guys,' he sighed, 'have to be careful how they handle women. We rarely know when we're about to step into deep shit, we don't even smell it until it's up to our chins. With Alex – maybe it's nothing. She'll kill me if I mess things up for her. But I'm worried, and I can't explain why. She's my sister: there's only she and me. We've had to look after each other. If I can ever help her, I always will. But she's not saying anything. And that is strange. It's strange, that she's got nothing to say.'

'Maybe she doesn't want your help. Maybe that's the reason she's not telling you anything.'

'Maybe,' he conceded. 'But I think she needs help, and she doesn't want to say why.'

I ashed my cigarette and said, 'She's got bruises on her arms.'

'I know. So we both know what we're talking about.'

'Guys are shits,' I muttered, and he acknowledged, 'Yes. Some.'

We looked away from one another, and I smoked my cigarette.

'If I help you,' I said eventually, 'I don't want to be excluded. Whatever you do, I want to be there. I want to know.'

Sasha laughed brokenly, lounged back in the couch. 'Louie,' he said, 'have you ever considered the possibility that there are some things you would rather not know?'

'I've considered it, and I've decided against it. I've lived long enough knowing nothing.'

'But you have a new life, now.'

'That's right.'

Sasha nodded slowly and I knew, having seen it before, that a nod was enough.

'OK,' I said. 'What do you want me to do?'

'Get the information. See if you can make her talk.'

'How am I supposed to do that?'

'If I could tell you how,' he said, 'I wouldn't need your help. You once told me you thought you were smart, but then you discovered you were average. Here is your chance to redeem yourself.'

I snorted, and he smiled. With the first touch of summer's sun his skin had darkened, his hair had streaked tawny, and he looked beautiful. He was beautiful like an animal, like a lion or a thoroughbred, trimmed down to streamlined essentials, with such a sense of strength beneath such an elegant frame. I had thought him beautiful, I knew, from the moment I had met him. It seemed a long time ago: I had been admiring from a distance for a long, long time. He gazed back at me, his fingers entwined; he was still, as if he knew I was watching, and everything I thought.

'You're not nice, are you,' I said.

'Not?' He arched an eyebrow. 'I was just about to offer you a biscuit, but you're not going to get one now.'

'I couldn't care one bit.'

'I don't believe you.'

I ditched my cigarette and he cocked his head when I glanced at him, both of us pretending we knew nothing, that we were just talking and teasing. I wavered, looked at the sleeping dog and the yellowed ceiling and my dirty fingernails, and when I glanced again at him, he smiled. He had lovely teeth. 'You've got lovely teeth,' I told him. 'Did your father do them? Or were you just born that way? Lucky.'

Sasha didn't answer; he stood, stepped over the coffee table, lifted me up from my chair and kissed me. His face was scratchy, because he hadn't shaved.

I didn't feel any guilt: I didn't feel one moment of guilt. Guilt would not have stopped me anyway. I had worked hard to reach that moment, and what I felt was rewarded, recognised. What I felt was a kind of soaring glory. His eyes glittered when he asked me, 'Don't you care?' and I answered, 'No. Do you?'

. . . Sometimes, when the weather is warm for the first time in such a long time and you realise that Christmas is approaching, that summer has come, and the afternoon shimmers and the birds don't sing and the day is like crystal, clear, and endless, I remember that day at Sasha's and his big dishevelled bed, how we languished on it for hours, stark naked and sweating, telling each other stories, drinking beer straight from the bottle, fanning our faces with our hands. I remember his body, how his skin was cool and how you could see the bones of his feet beneath it, and the veins in his hands, I remember how he slept with his head on his arms, his breath fluttering strands of hair. I remember the windows, the carpet, the walls, I remember the floating sound of voices in the garden and how Sasha took me in his arms as if I might otherwise run from the noise, and I remember the feeling of safety, safe as if we weren't even there to be seen, the safety of the gods. The memory almost sinks me, stops me in my tracks, creates a joyful, wistful swoop inside. I died and went to Heaven that day; no day has ever come close to equalling it, and none is so carefully preserved in my mind. I would not have cared if I really had died, and Sasha had died alongside me, at some point when we slept a while. I would have been satisfied that I had lived enough. And sometimes, when it's a balmy summer's afternoon and Christmas is in the air, I want to phone him up and say, *Sasha, remember* – but that might spoil everything, and I fear that he's forgotten. We never talked about it afterwards. Yet his memory was a good one: when, at dusk, I slung my bag to go, I turned to him in the doorway and said, 'That *was* you on the train with the blind man, wasn't it?' and he answered, 'Well, you know, it might have been.'

I don't regret; not then, when things had yet to happen, not now, when everything has.

Flynn was willing enough to go with me but he was relentlessly curious and asked, 'Why don't you take Andy?'

I looked at him, Flynn, who had shown me his meek treasures and had conjured himself a better past. Maturity had not settled on Flynn, and maybe it simply could not. There was something of the child's doll about him: it was rare to see him unsmiling and his limbs seemed unusually supple, as if he could bend them any way. The light slanting through the train window showed up the blond hairs on his cheeks, the downy, futile wish for a moustache. His sandy hair was floppy and cowlicked and his green eyes were round, cheerful, clear. It must often have been the perfect disguise, for his face was the face of someone simpler, different. I probably could have confided in Flynn. I could have explained that an integrity I'd assumed was inside me, strong enough to guide me, had fizzled under its first testing, and that although I was appalled and ashamed I was *happy*, I couldn't describe how pleased I was with myself. I could have said that the place Andy once occupied was now arid and deserted, that I'd conquered higher ground and when I looked down I did so with fondness and faint sadness but no shreds of remorse. I could have told him that Sasha was the first thing I thought of upon waking, the last thing I thought of before falling asleep . . . I could have said I knew a secret. But I did not know what Flynn would say about that, and I was not sure I wanted his opinion, so I said, 'You're the best. You're the king.'

This he accepted, but he insisted, 'I'm not going to do it for you. You've seen me do it enough to know how.'

But I had not: I'd been present, all eyes and astonishment, but I had never seen. I shifted in my seat, frightened, determined to be brave. I knew he would help me if I needed him to. I watched him watching a gang of clean happy boys and we listened to their conversation, heard the words *scavenger hunt* and *youth group* and *God*. They'd been driven blindfolded to the outskirts of suburbia and now they were making their way to the city, where they would follow clues and collect the dozen required objects, a pamphlet from the Tourist Centre, a map of the Botanic Gardens, a ticket to the Museum . . . They would delegate, disperse, regroup with their hands full . . . they'd race back, when they had everything, to the place of rendezvous, and if they were fast enough they would win, win, win we didn't hear what . . . We listened to their talk and too-loud laughter and Flynn swivelled his eyes to me. 'What is the point of it?' he asked. 'What's the point?' The train carriage emptied at the last of the stations and we went our ancient, separate ways, us thieves and those god-boys.

We went to the bookshop that Flynn favoured when in need of a present for his scholarly Nanna. It was the most prestigious and snootiest bookshop in the city and we stopped outside the window while Flynn peered through the glass. 'Hmm,' he said. 'Felicity. She has an eagle's eye.'

'Oh, no . . .'

'You'll be fine. Hold my hand. Couples aren't so suspicious.'

I took his hand and he winced. 'Nervous, are we?' he asked, and grappled with my sweaty palm. He leaned against the door and I followed him through.

The shop was cool and tasteful. The carpet was thick and olive, the shelves were glass and ranged to the ceiling. There was a choir singing from lofty speakers but few browsers around to hear it on this hot weekend morning. The woman behind the counter wore a badge with her name printed on it, *Felicity*, and she looked up at us, her face as mild and kindly as a spaniel's. 'Good morning,' she said.

Flynn piped, 'Hello.'

She smiled shyly at me and returned to flipping through her paperwork. 'Do not be deceived,' warned Flynn.

The art books were arranged at the rear of the shop and we made our way down to them, me holding tight to Flynn's bony hand. When he lingered I dragged him forward, not wanting to be there forever, until he scowled at me and said, 'Dearest, we came here to *look*.'

So we looked, Flynn convincingly at the books, me covertly at Felicity. She glanced up regularly from her place near the register, scanning the customers and the shelves, and the gentleness in her face, when she did so, was replaced with something else: the deliberate look of someone like her looking for someone like me. She caught my eye once, and I jerked a ghastly grin to my face.

'Sweety,' Flynn said quietly, not lifting his eyes from a book, 'why are you acting so bizarrely?'

'Flynn, let's get out of here, I can't do this – '

'Yeah you can.'

'Can't you distract her?'

'We don't need to do that.'

'Please – '

'Remember, class and confidence, creamcake. Keep your voice down.'

He shelved the book and we drifted closer to the art section, the choir wailing above us, my fingers clenching his. I glimpsed the book I knew I wanted, my literary grail, glossy and solid on the shelf. 'Go on,' he urged.

I stared at the thing: it seemed monolithic, so unwieldy, so unwilling to budge. 'I'm scared,' I breathed.

'It's easy,' he said, as quietly as if he'd only thought the words.

I raised my arm: to my horror, it struck at the air like a puppet's, and fell to my side like a dead thing. Flynn exploded into laughter and the noise ricocheted around the shop's tall walls. Felicity spun in her sensible shoes and stared in our direction. 'Shut up!' I gasped at him.

Flynn covered his mouth, his eyes crinkled into emerald crescents. I pulled my hand from his grip and looked around frantically, sure that everyone was listening, that Felicity had pegged us for what we were and was this minute ringing the police, that we'd leave with a uniformed escort and the whole city would stop to watch. 'We'll come tomorrow,' I whimpered, every trace of bravery wrung out of me. 'I'll do it tomorrow – '

'No. We're here now.'

'We'll get sprung, Flynn! She knows what we're doing, she knows why we're here! Look, I'll pay for it – just let me pay for it – '

'Don't be ridiculous,' he said sharply, no longer so amused. His eyes flickered around the shop, skimming the customers and Felicity and me, and I saw impatience jump in his jaw. 'You know how to do this. Pick it up, put it in your bag, piss off.'

'I can't! I won't!'

Flynn glared. The habitual expression of innocence was cleanly gone from his face. In one swift movement, without checking on Felicity, he reached to the shelf and brought the book down, yanked open my backpack and dumped the book inside. The weight of it jarred my shoulders and I stepped back once and then again, not taking my eyes from him. I saw what I had not seen before: I understood that he did not give up, that obstacles in the path of his determination were swept aside by whatever means came to hand. I had proved myself an obstacle and he had stepped over me, casting a shadow of black contempt. And then his face changed instantly, and he was the old Flynn again. 'Come on,' he said, brusque but not bullying. He held out his hand for mine and I let him take it. The door seemed impossibly distant and Flynn made me walk slowly all the way. He gave Felicity a quick and polite departing nod and she said, 'Goodbye.'

Outside, we ducked down the first laneway we found. I slumped on the bluestone and threw off the backpack. Flynn hesitated before crouching beside me in the gutter, his wrists resting on his knees. He said, 'That went quite well, I thought.'

'Shut up!'

'What's the matter?'

I clutched handfuls of my hair, my heart pounding so fiercely I feared it would self-destruct, would punch through my chest and bounce down the laneway like some gruesome softball. 'I changed my mind!' I shouted at him. 'I changed my mind and you didn't care, you were pressuring me! Why did you have to laugh?'

'Well, it was funny – '

'It was not! If you had left me alone – '

'If I'd left you alone you would have got nothing.'

I buried my face in my hands, hunching as tight as I could. 'I might have, if you hadn't laughed. I couldn't think properly after you laughed . . .'

'Don't pretend you would have done it,' he said, 'because you wouldn't have, you couldn't. You didn't change your mind, you wimped out.'

I gave up trying to deny it. 'You said it would be easy,' I moaned, 'but it was horrible. God, what if she'd caught us?'

'She didn't, though. And if she had, so what?'

I cringed at the idea of such humiliation and Flynn saw and understood. 'If a bit of embarrassment is going to kill you,' he said, 'you're not going to get very far.'

'Far in *what*?' I yelped, furious at him. 'Far in a pathetic little life of crime like yours?'

'Far in anything,' he replied placidly. 'Definitely not far in a life of crime. You have to be brave for that.'

'Brave!' I screeched, wanting to gouge his eyes out. 'It was *me* who saved your arse at the police station!'

'By *crying*.'

'So what! I didn't hear you complain. And it was *me* who chased off the neighbour at Elliot's house, have you forgotten that?'

'So you're a good liar.' Flynn shrugged. 'Lots of people are. You don't need anything but a smart mouth to be a good liar. To do what we do, you've got to have *guts*. You can't wimp out every time something happens that you don't want happening. You think it's like a game, Louie, and sometimes it is and sometimes it isn't, but it's not a game you'll always win because you're a girl or because you're cute or because you can turn on the tears. That mightn't save you when you most need saving. There's people around who'll hurt you *because* you are a girl. There's people who will kick cuteness to bits. There's people who'll get off on seeing you cry. You mightn't *get* to tell lies to them because every one of your teeth will be lying in the dirt in front of you. There's people who genuinely don't care if they live or die, and they certainly won't care if you do or not. What are you going to do if you meet one of them one day, Louie?'

I stared down at the cobbles. 'I don't know,' I sighed. 'How can you beat someone like that?'

'You can't, not really. The only chance you've got is by *being* someone like that.'

'. . . I'm not, though.'

'No. And you shouldn't want to be.'

I picked up a stone and flung it away. 'I wanted to be brave,' I said. 'I was trying.'

'Yeah, I know.'

'But I'm not cut out for a life of delinquency.'

'No.'

'You're right, that's all I am. A good liar.'

'Hmm.'

'That's something, though,' I said, hopefully. 'Isn't it?'

'Well,' he said, 'I suppose it's handy.'

I hung my head, mortally discouraged. That was what I was, an accomplished liar. And something about that reeked of being the lowest of the low.

Flynn had lit a cigarette and was fishing in my backpack. I

watched from the corner of my eye. 'What are you looking for?' I asked eventually.

'You've got a lot of junk in here. This.' He extracted a paperback and propped it on his knees. I'd never seen the book before. It wasn't mine. I didn't ask how it had got in my backpack, this book I'd never owned or seen before, price sticker still attached. He stroked the novel's cover and flipped it to read the blurb, smiling, very pleased with this prize. As I watched him, I felt grateful to and charmed by my superior in crime. You could trust Flynn, I believed, with the life you had no desire to lose; he was like some misguided guardian angel. 'I'd yell for you,' I said.

He looked up, squinting. 'What?'

'If I met someone who wasn't impressed with my lies,' I said. 'I'd yell for you.'

'Oh,' he said, 'OK.'

I almost told him about Sasha and me, I wanted to, but I didn't. It didn't seem the moment to hammer out the morality of ditching one's boyfriend in favour of that boyfriend's best friend. Instead, I smacked him on the back and said, 'Come on, sweety, let's go.'

I knocked on the front door, the first time I'd ever done so, and it was answered by Sasha himself. I hadn't expected to see him and he seemed disconcerted to see me. He paused and said flatly, 'Hello.'

'Hi.'

We looked at each other; I smiled, and he shifted his footing, hooked his fingers around the handle of the door. It struck me as touching, that he should be bashful.

'I've come to see Alexandra,' I explained.

'Oh, I see. Come in.' He swung the door and waved me inside. I followed him through the sprawling house until we reached the foot of the stairs. 'Alex!' he called. 'Someone's here to see you.'

'How are you, Sash?' I asked.

He turned to me, hands on his hips. 'Fine.'

Alexandra appeared at the top of the stairs and when I next glanced to Sasha, he had gone. 'Alexandra,' I said, proffering my parcel, 'I've got a present for you.'

'For me?' She frowned. 'What for?'

'For the bowl.'

She came down the staircase glidingly, barely lifting her feet. 'That was a gift,' she said as she reached me. 'You didn't need to buy me anything.'

'I know – I didn't – '

She placed the parcel on a sideboard and undid the ribbon, revealing the hardbacked history of art. 'You've probably got one already,' I said.

'Not this one. It's lovely, Louie.'

She seemed sincere and I was pleased, but my work was far from done. 'Well,' I said, 'I suppose I should go.'

'Don't be silly,' Alex said obligingly. 'Stay for a cup of coffee.'

She made coffee in the vast white kitchen, and we took our cups outside to the pool deck: she sat on a shaded bench, and I sat where I could dangle my fingertips in the water. Jemima, all golden hair and fringed waving tail, ambled across the grass to be near us. I saw the four-wheel drive parked in front of the bungalow and a pile of garden clippings that someone had painstakingly raked. Alexandra sniffed the air and said, 'I love the smell of summer – I love everything about summer. The world is a different place.'

'Yeah,' I said. This opportunity, once blown, would not come easily again, and the weather leads nowhere. But then Alexandra asked after Andy, and I saw my chance. I offered up my relationship to get what I wanted, a sacrifice to Sasha.

'I guess he's OK,' I said. 'I haven't seen him much, lately.'

Alex creased her faultless brow. 'What's the matter?'

'Oh, I don't know . . . We tried. We don't fight or anything like that. But it's like – we don't have much to say to each other. I don't think we really *interest* each other. It was good at first and it's still good sometimes, but it's sort of . . . faded. At least for me. We haven't talked about it but I think he feels it too.' I tugged at the laces of my runners, striving for poignancy. 'I don't see him every day any more, like I did at the start,' I said. 'We don't phone each other just to say hello. We go out without each other. And we don't care.'

'There's nothing more wretched than a failing relationship,' mused Alexandra. 'It's like a bird with a broken wing, fluttering and stumbling and trying to get off the ground, but inside it knows it's doomed.'

'That's exactly how it feels,' I said. 'Doomed. But not in a tragic way. I like him, I'll always like him. I want to stay friends with him, and with his friends. It just needs to end; we'll be happier when it ends. At the moment we're stuck, wasting time. Neither of us wants to be the one who actually says the final words, so it's lingering. Like some annoying old relative who won't cooperate and die.'

'Guys are notorious for not breaking up a relationship. They have no gumption for that sort of thing. You'll have to do it, Louie.'

I nodded, squinting over the glittering swimming pool. 'I guess so . . . It will be sad, though. He's the first guy I've ever gone out with.'

'I think the first boyfriend always suffers for what he teaches you.'

I looked at her. 'Does he? Why?'

'You know things now that you didn't know before you met him,' she said simply. 'If you're not madly in love with him, of course you're going to get restless. You want to try your tricks on someone else. Were you ever madly in love with him?'

'I'm not sure,' I said. 'Before I got him, I loved things about him. I loved to catch a glimpse of him, to hear him talking, to watch him walking around. I loved *imagining* him, imagining the conversations we'd have, where we'd go and what we'd do. When I got him it was like a dream, like winning a competition, and I loved *that*. And now it's just part of my life, it seems so ordinary, so everyday. You're right – I want to be free, to try my tricks. But first we have to end it and I don't know what to say.'

She lifted her chin and announced, 'Andy, you've served your purpose, now bugger off.'

'Andy, been nice knowing you, now I'm bored to death.'

We chuckled. 'Poor Andy,' I said.

She shook her head; she had the same lazy curls as her brother but she wore them longer, and they jangled past her shoulders. 'Poor Andy nothing,' she said shortly. 'You say you both see the end approaching: he will be as relieved as you'll be, to end it. He might pretend otherwise, he might cultivate a broken heart because it's handy to have one of those, they're very alluring, but guys are resilient. They're so convinced of their own attractions that they bounce back like rubber balls. You'll both be delighted with the decision. You can open a bottle of champagne.'

'You're terrible, Alex.'

'Not at all, I'm a realist. Do you have your arrows aimed at anyone else?'

The question startled me, and Alexandra narrowed her eyes. 'Sashy?' she asked.

'I don't know – Sasha – well, yeah. Yeah, I like Sasha. He's nice.'

'Sasha's lovely,' she agreed. 'But you don't want him. He's not right for you.'

'Why not?'

'This is your *life*, Louie,' she said. 'Try not to make choices that will make you miserable.'

I shifted, pretending it was the decking that was uncomfortable. She was speaking through a wisdom that I would put faith in only after I learned it for myself. I was young; and when I needed to I could act my age. 'Do you have a boyfriend?' I asked.

Alexandra hesitated, sat back in the shade. '*Boyfriend*,' she sighed.

'That's such a sappy word. I suppose I do. There's this guy I've been seeing for a few months.'

'What's his name?'

'Daniel.'

'Daniel who?'

'Daniel Falconer.'

I repeated it to myself: *Falconer, Daniel*. 'I hope he looks as flash as his name.'

'He does. He's one of the best-looking guys I've ever seen.'

'I would love to go out with someone gorgeous. You'd feel so proud.'

Alexandra smiled dimly. 'No you wouldn't,' she said. 'You'd be full of doubts, like me. Everywhere you went, you'd hear people thinking, How did *she* get *him*? . . . Anyway, all the good-looking guys that I've known have been bad in bed. Ugly ones are better. Maybe because they've spent a lifetime having to try harder to impress.'

I giggled, and she smiled into her cup. I asked, 'If he fills you with doubts and he's bad in bed, why are you going out with him?'

She looked wry, lifting her shoulders. 'I don't know. He has an unusual way of looking at life.'

'How old is he?'

'He's twenty-seven.'

'Alex!' I breathed. Such an age sounded inconceivably ancient to me. Alexandra, I knew, was twenty-four, and even that seemed perilously close to decrepitude. She gave me a tolerant smile and ran a hand along Jemima's coat. 'Is he rich?' I asked. 'Where does he live?'

'He rents a terrace in Carlton. He's not rich, no. He's a student, like you.'

'Studying?'

'Law.'

I nodded, stashing the information away. 'And you get along well? Better than Andy and me?'

'Sometimes. Like you, I don't think it will last.'

'Why not?'

'It just – won't.'

'But you'll stay friends with him?'

'. . . Some of them,' she said, 'you know you'll never see again, once it's finished.'

She sighed, not unhappily, and I could see she was closing the door on the matter. No doubt I'd taken up enough of her time; I was only Sasha's friend, quaintly willing to listen and learn, but young and silly and, in the end, a limited source of amusement. I'd have to go soon, and the traitor in me did not yet have all it needed.

'Those bruises on your arms,' I said, 'did he do that to you?'

I expected her to ignore me or to baulk at my impertinence, but she did neither. Like an erring child she jutted her lower lip, cast her eyes down and peeped, 'Yes.'

My mouth fell open and I gaped like a fish. 'Does he do – things like that – often?'

'No. Not often. He just forgets that he's stronger than me, sometimes. He doesn't mean it.'

'He doesn't *mean* it? He often, accidentally, hurts you? How can you say he doesn't *mean* it?'

'He doesn't, that's why.'

'How can you *stay* with him? How can you possibly *like* him?'

'Be quiet, Louie!' she flared. 'Keep your voice down. You don't understand.'

I struggled to collect myself before she lost her temper and walked away. 'I'm sorry,' I said. 'It's none of my business, I know. But – Alex – he shouldn't be hurting you. You know it, but you're letting it happen anyway – '

'I'm not *letting* it happen, he doesn't have my *permission*.'

I stared at her, crouched in the shade like some cornered, angry animal. The coffee had gone cloudy in my cup and the heat of the sun was piercing my clothes. For a minute the only sound was the panting of Jemima and the gurgling of the pool's filter. Alexandra eventually cleared her throat and said, 'I hit him back sometimes, anyway.'

I cast my eyes over her; she was lightly built and slender; she wouldn't know how to hit, to make it hurt.

'I broke some of his stuff too, on purpose,' she said, and laughed feebly. 'He doesn't have it all his own way.'

She must have realised how pathetic she sounded: she ducked back into the shade and her fingers fluttered nervously. She did not speak again until a few moments had gone by.

'Don't worry about it, Louie,' she said.

'Don't worry? How am I meant to not worry?'

'I'm going to deal with it.'

'When?' I asked. 'How?'

She lifted a finger to her lips and I shut my mouth. She told me, 'Don't say anything to anyone, all right?'

'Why not?'

'Because I've asked you not to. I want to deal with this properly.'

'He needs gentle handling, does he? Poor guy.'

'Louie.'

For a minute I could not bring myself to speak. I was sweating with disgust and fury. Then, employing my single talent for lies, I said, 'All right. I won't tell.'

My fingers were twined very tight around the handle of my coffee cup and I had to prise them free. Making a promise I intended to break caused me no qualms; it never had, and it certainly wouldn't now. Whether or not I kept the matter confidential was something not only out of Alex's hands, but something that had never been within her reach. She had no right to beg silence from me, the request was not hers to make. I would tell Sasha not because I had plotted to tell Sasha but because men should not hurt women, and people like Daniel Falconer deserve what happens to them, whatever hard fate comes to find them, once the truth is dug up and exposed. When Alexandra left the decking carrying the mugs and with Jemima trotting after her, it was all I could do not to run screaming to Sasha's bungalow and spill the information like black coals across the carpet.

I think it is getting late now. A shadow has come into the room, angling across the floor with a fine edge to it, like a clean cut. A whole afternoon has whittled away while we've been sitting here: hours of my life, though not wasted.

Alexandra looks at her brother. She says, in a voice that shows she's just now realising it, 'You used her.'

Sasha looks at his sister. 'Only to help you,' he says. 'It didn't hurt her. She was quite happy to do it. It made her feel important.'

'You sent a spy.'

'The ends justify the means.'

'What if I hadn't told her anything? What if I'd taken the book and walked away?'

Sasha smiles. 'But that didn't happen,' he says. 'For a start, you are not that impolite. And Louie had a talent for sucking information out of people.'

'That's true,' nods Alex. 'I'd sworn not to tell anyone, but I told her. She was so horrified. I told her the truth: I really was going to finish it, I was just waiting for the right time. Louie didn't believe me, but I had decided.'

She will leave under an acid rain of abuse, she supposes, and she'll be branded with the words Daniel burns into most of his previous girlfriends. Bitch, slut, slag. He will never thank her for her company.

Nothing special has happened to bring her to this decision. He has not been nasty once too often. The wad of rejection letters has not become a sliver too thick for her liking. She's good at fending off the questions her parents ask about Daniel, things haven't become complicated on that front. No: it's just that it seems her old self, the self she'd been before she met Daniel, has reappeared, and is stunned to discover how far she's fallen in its absence. It has reasserted itself, perhaps in her sleep. It has said, Enough.

'Everyone gets stepped on by life,' she has told Daniel. 'Everyone gets disappointed. Everyone fails and gets hurt. That doesn't mean everyone takes it out on other people.'

'What do you mean?' he had asked. 'How do I take it out on anyone? Alexandra? What are you talking about?'

She doesn't believe his perplexity. He means to do the things he does. When he grabs her hands and uses them to slap her own face, when he goes icy silent and stays that way until she's frantic at the thought of what's coming next, that is Daniel doing those things. Not the rejection letters, not the

Troubled Background, not some other, unruly personality, not a mythical demon inside: *him*. *He* does that. He likes doing it. He is not going to stop doing it. So she will put a stop to it being done to her, but she will let him down gently. She will wait until Christmas has passed, for she has no desire to spoil that day for him. There have been good times between them and she does not want to think of him sitting alone while everyone else celebrates. And she knows, too, that she has also done wrong. She has burdened Daniel with her dream and encouraged him to take it on as his own, but it never was his, and he never wanted it to be. The country is an option for him, not a goal. But she has pinned her dream on him, and stayed with him long after she's started to hate him, in the desperate hope that the transplant will take. He has been stalked by her neediness, her need to have someone accompany her along her path, a neediness that would tolerate just about anything, if only it could be satisfied. He will say that she's used him, and he will be right, and that will mean he is not completely in the wrong.

Still – she could weep. Not for him, and the life she knows he's going to live – for the dream. It has come, for a short time, so tantalisingly close.

But, her old self reminds her, that has been a faulty replica of the dream, one that would come with a sting in its tail. For her, living in the country is meant to be a thing of joy: dreams are, by their nature, things of joy. Life in the country with

Daniel would not be like that. That life raced toward a single scene: she sees herself fleeing in the dead of night, a fretful child buckled into the seat beside her, and Alexandra driving as fast as she can but glancing in the mirrors to see headlights coming closer, closer. No: that is not what she wants from life. That is not what she will give herself. She will hold on to the dream, and one day she might fulfil it – but it will be, now, a dream that has been treated roughly, and she wonders if it will show signs of that abuse.

'Why isn't life cleaner?' she asks us. 'Why isn't it fairer? Why is it so shitty so much of the time? It pisses me off.'

'You need to exercise tighter control,' her brother tells her. 'Don't be a player, be the one who writes the rules.'

'That's easy for you to say, Sasha,' Kate says to him. 'Most people don't live a life like yours. Most of us fumble along alone, rather than rule our own empire.'

It makes me blink; I've never thought of myself as being part of an empire. We're friends, that's all. An empire. Run by Sasha. God.

'It so happens,' says Alexandra, looking her brother in the eye, 'that I *had* decided to exercise tighter control. I'd made up my mind. I was going to get rid of him, just like I told Louie. And we know what happened next, don't we?'

We did.

Sasha Johns rallied his forces on hearing my news. He called in favours from everyone who owed him one. I'd provided him with much of what he needed – a name, a vicinity, a reason – and it was an easy thing for Alexandra's boyfriend to be traced; others lent their time to watching him, discovering his habits, gauging the likelihood of alterations, surprises, disasters. Alexandra herself was watched, and careful note was taken of the times she was most likely to go visiting. Things moved with the sleekness that comes from years of practice and fine-tuning, deliberately, without undue haste but also without delay. There would be no mistakes this time, no cars breaking down, no flesh cut open; the plan, essentially simple, would be organised into glassy perfection. It was flawless and ready to unfurl as soon as the call came, and it came close to midnight, a week before Christmas. One of Sasha's acquaintances, sitting in a car parked directly opposite Daniel Falconer's house, observing that the street was quiet and that Daniel was alone, judged that this was the time to act.

Andy and Flynn were at the bungalow, and so was I. It was not the first time since my afternoon with Sasha that I had been in the presence of Sasha and Andy together but such meetings still filled me with an edgy anxiety, as if the truth skulked around the walls and might at any instant leap to the centre of the room, bright as fire and bawling what it knew. But such meetings were thrilling, too, brimming with anticipation and nerves; I watched closely for the moment Sasha's eyes alighted on my face and then I would give him a covert smile, which he was too discreet to acknowledge. If he wanted to preserve the secrecy a while, I was happy to go along with his plans. So I would sit between the pair of them, Andy and Sasha Johns, and chat away pointlessly, revelling in the knowledge that not only was I welcome here, but that I had successfully entangled myself.

The bleating of the mobile phone interrupted my monologue, and we watched as Sasha retrieved the machine and flipped its cover open. He listened to the words of the caller, contributing nothing himself. Then he put the phone down and said, 'We're going.'

'It's on?' I asked. 'Daniel?'

'Louie,' said Andy, reaching for his boots, 'you better go home.'

'No,' I said, 'no, no. I'm coming with you.'

Sasha was already on his feet, gathering his wallet and keys. Flynn had rung up Hastings and was mumbling into the mobile phone. Andy yanked on a boot and said, 'You should stay here.'

'Sasha said that if I found out the things you needed to know, then I could come with you. So I did and I am.'

Andy tisked, and frowned at Sasha. 'What did you say that for?'

Sasha swung round and looked at us. 'Said what?' he asked impatiently. 'What did I say?'

'That Louie could come with us tonight.'

'I never said that.'

'Yes you did,' I said. 'You know you did.'

'When?' Sasha shot back. 'When did I say that?'

I stared at him; Flynn had closed the mobile and was looking at me, and Andy was too. But I was staring at Sasha, and he was staring at me.

'You know very well when,' I said softly.

'No,' he said. 'It's quite escaped my memory.'

For a moment I was silent. The look on his face was dead. I knew what he was doing; I felt things sliding from my grasp. I dammed the slide as best I could: I asked, 'Will I remind you?'

'Go ahead,' he replied instantly. 'You realise, of course, that we have an audience. Your boyfriend, for instance.'

I think I gasped, as if for air, for the room itself became airless, its oxygen scorched by the revelation which bounded to the centre of the room and which Flynn and Andy spotted at once, which made them recoil. I myself saw nothing, but heard a thumping in my ears. Sasha stood and stared at me steadily but I wasn't seeing him; I'd never really see him again. I wasn't looking at Andy, either, but I heard him cough on a laugh. He laughed – startled, but not angry, and why would he be: he could forgive Sasha everything, but he had few ties to me, because I had been severing them one by one.

Apart from me, Flynn was the only one who seemed aghast. He blinked and blinked and stared at me.

'Jesus, Sasha,' said Andy. He said it lightly, shaking his head, as if he'd just heard a bad, but sickly funny, joke. He reached for the other boot and pulled it on. 'I'd hate to see how you treat your enemies.'

Flynn just cocked his head and gazed at me.

'Are we going?' asked Sasha, irritably.

The three of us stood, me rising to my feet like a zombie. I knew I should leave, run and never be seen again, but the part of me that had worked so hard to bring me to this night was refusing to let go. Sasha didn't care for me: perhaps he hated me. I had betrayed and humiliated Andy and he had hardly cared. Some image of me that Flynn had created had been smeared, and he could not even speak to me. Everything was destroyed, the damage was bloody and jagged and my face was burning, my world was crashing – yet still I would not walk away. If I went with them, maybe we could start again. Maybe the business, and the bonds the business made, could pull us through this clean. The business was a thing that could render this scene trivial.

Flynn drove and we travelled in silence. It was a week night, a dark night and warm, so we kept the windows down. I remember the wind slashing my hair and the terrible, freezing hollowness inside me. That I was there in the car, that I'd achieved what I wanted, didn't matter, and it didn't matter that we were closing in on an actual man, a man who couldn't hear us coming but would remember this night for the rest of his life. What mattered was the fact that I had wrecked everything, that I felt stricken and disjoined, and I was filled with the need to see someone punished for all of it, for hands that hurt, for words that wound, for looks that kill and loves that don't last and for all the flimsy dreams that have ever fallen through. I sought revenge for people like Alexandra, and for stupid people like me.

Hastings was waiting for us outside the house, Chopper at his heels and a toolbox in his hand. The person who had placed the call on the mobile phone was sitting on a fence across the road; he nodded to us, and Sasha nodded back. None of us spoke. In the shadow of the truck we wriggled our fingers into gloves and Hastings produced hats and scarves. I tried to copy what Flynn was doing and wrapped the scarf around my mouth and nose, jammed the hat on my head. Sasha pulled on a balaclava and with a baseball bat in his hand he looked like someone who would terrify me, someone whose attention you would dread. Flynn came up to me and all I could see were his emerald eyes: he seemed to want to say something and I asked roughly, 'What?'

He stepped back immediately. 'Nothing,' he said.

'Ready?' Sasha asked.

We walked through Daniel Falconer's gate, climbed up the steps and gathered on the veranda. Sasha rapped on the door with the end of the baseball bat and for a moment we waited. My heart knocked at my chest once, twice, again. Then the door was unlocked from the inside and Hastings gave it a mighty shove, wrenching it from the man's grip, sending it slamming to the wall. We walked into the hallway, driving the man backward, and Flynn locked the door behind us.

'I'm sure you don't know us,' Sasha began. He spoke quietly and would do so the whole time we were there, so the man had to listen intently. 'We are acquainted with Alexandra Johns, and we disapprove of the way you treat her.'

The man lurched backwards all the way down the hall, Sasha treading in his footsteps. His hands rose, now and then, as if to wipe us from his sight. His mouth was open but nothing was coming out. When we reached the lounge-room and the walls widened around us he finally found his voice to say, 'Get out of my house.'

Flynn chuckled. Then he produced a switchblade and sliced the cord of the telephone. The man staggered to see him do it, rocking on his heels. Sasha glanced about the room, the baseball bat propped over his shoulder. He said, 'What a pleasant house you have.'

The man licked his lips, tore his eyes from Flynn and the knife. '. . . What?'

'I'm admiring your house, Daniel. Very nice. Very homely. I expected something different, I guess, from one such as yourself.'

Daniel, rigid in the centre of the room, seemed undecided what to say. He was as handsome as Alexandra had made him out to be: he was tall and willowy, his flitting eyes were a deep blue, and his hair was thick and jet-black. But his pretty face was nothing, it showed nothing of who he was, it was a mask as effective as the ones we wore. Ours showed our intention, but not us; his showed fear and outrage, but it didn't show him. We had evidently woken him from dozing, for he looked dishevelled and dazed. He wore nothing but a pair of navy satin boxer shorts and his legs were thin and hairy, his chest was knobby with bone.

'I thought you'd live – I don't know – in a hovel,' Sasha continued. 'In some sort of pit or sink. But you don't. You live here, all by yourself, surrounded by thick cream walls. How about that.'

Hastings was standing like a totem beside Sasha, the toolbox swaying in his grip. Flynn had disappeared. Andy was walking the perimeter of the room, reading the messages on the Christmas cards and examining the ornaments. Chopper sat in the middle of the floor and was listening closely. I had stopped in the doorway and didn't move from there. Daniel's eyes went to each of us but would dart back, over and over, to the toolbox in Hastings's hand.

Sasha sniffed. 'You should live in the gutter, shouldn't you, Danny boy.'

'I'm expecting visitors,' the man spluttered. 'They'll be here any second.'

'Really? They'll get a surprise, won't they, when you don't answer the door. *Where can he be?* they'll ask themselves, and they'll knock and knock again. *That Dan*, they'll say, *you just can't trust him*. And you can't, can you, Dan?'

'I'd like you to leave, now.'

Sasha sighed deeply. 'What you'd like,' he said tranquilly, 'is of no consequence. Shall I tell you what we like? We like harming evil little fuckers like yourself. Nasty, stunted little turds who haven't the balls to hit a man but don't mind giving a woman a whack or two. Tiny, whining, prickless little reptiles who feel good when they hurt a woman, who feel tough when they frighten a girl, who love the sound of crying, the sound of something breaking. Fetid, odious little shits like you, who've always got an excuse for what they do but never really tell the truth. You never say, I do this because it's all I can do. I do this because I'm weak. I do it because it gives me a hard-on, it helps me jack off.'

Daniel said, 'Get out!' and Sasha swung the baseball bat.

I hadn't thought he was close enough to connect, but the bat caught Daniel in the ribcage and made a muffled sound. Daniel dropped immediately to the floor. 'Be quiet,' was all Sasha said to him.

Daniel writhed and groaned on the polished boards, heaving and jolting. Chopper darted to him and made snipping grabs at his hair until Hastings pulled him away. Beyond Daniel's noise we could hear the sound of Flynn ferreting somewhere in the house. Sasha, Andy and Hastings stared silently at the man at their feet and I knew they were waiting for him to recover; they needed him to recover.

'We're not here to play with you,' Sasha told him, when Daniel had ceased to drag his breaths and lay still and curved. 'I hope you see that we are not here to mess around.'

Daniel sniffed; he quivered. He looked pathetic on the floor, small.

'Get up, now.'

He looked like he might refuse, but perhaps he saw himself, and he got to his feet, hunched by the pain in his ribs.

'Stand against the wall.'

'No.'

'. . . I beg your pardon?'

Daniel's lips trembled. 'No,' he said again.

Hastings lashed out his empty hand and the man rocketed to the wall, smacking his knuckles and skull. Chopper barked, his snout wrinkled and shivering. Daniel made a string of whimpering sounds and his fear made him furious; he bit his lip, tossed his head and pounded his fists against the wall. 'Look,' he cried, 'I'm sorry! Whatever I've done, I'm sorry for doing it! Leave now, and I promise I'll tell Alexandra I don't want to see her again. And I won't, I won't – '

'You won't,' Sasha agreed. 'But that doesn't heal the harm that's already been done, does it? And that won't keep other women safe from you, will it? We want to be sure we don't have to pay you another visit, Dan. Lift your arms. Hold your hands flat to the wall.'

The man lifted his arms from his sides and Andy sneered, 'What does the cunt think he is, a fucking martyr?'

'Not like Jesus, Dan,' Sasha said patiently. 'Bend your elbows.'

He did, sliding his fingers along the plaster, and his position became one of surrender.

'Shall I explain what we're going to do to you?' Sasha asked him. 'Or should I just show you what's in the toolbox and let you figure it out for yourself? What do you prefer, hmm? You've gone very quiet, Dan. I bet you're not so quiet when you're about to smash

Alexandra across the room. I bet you've got plenty to say for yourself then . . . Do you know what I think, Dan?'

The man shook his head, strands of his hair catching on the wall.

'I think I'll show you what's in the toolbox,' said Sasha.

Hastings placed the box on the floor and unlatched it. Inside was the Ramset gun. Daniel stared at it with a ghastly wonder, a thing he'd never seen before, so large and solid and silver, and yet something so obviously a gun, so evidently capable of harm. I knew what it was: I knew it could drive a nail through steel. 'Oh,' I said, 'no.'

Sasha glanced at me, tightening his grip on the baseball bat. 'You can't,' I said.

'Daniel,' said Sasha, looking back to the man, 'have you met Louie? She's the one who arranged our visit tonight. I'd have to tell you that, without her help, we wouldn't be here.'

I wanted to fly at him, to tear the balaclava from his head and rip his eyes from his skull. It would have taken only the use of his name – just those small words, *Sasha Johns* – and his mask would have been stripped from him, the entire plan sent haywire, and the gaping, aching core of myself would have wreaked a fine vengeance, but at that moment I chose to stay silent. And I still wonder why: whether my lips were sealed by fear, or by a stubborn loyalty.

Flynn chose that moment to stroll into the room. 'Well!' he chirped brightly. 'I've got to say, Danny, I wouldn't mind a place like this myself. Nice clean bathroom, plenty of shelves for your allergy medicine. Nice big bed, great for jumping up and down on. Nice clean sheets, good squishy pillows. Lots of cupboard space for your clothes. I notice you've got your clothes organised according to their colour, white shirts together, black socks together, all of that, and I think I might have messed it up a bit, sorry. There was one drawer I couldn't open so I had to, sort of, well, break the lock, and all I found was a diary. Why do you keep your diary locked up? Personally I find that a bit vain. There's nothing in it worth reading anyway, is there? I like your study, I think that's my favourite room. All your papers and things, your letters, very interesting. That little security box where you keep your passport and your birth certificate, very sensible. And those photos of yourself on the hallway walls, very sweet. So handy in case you forget who you are. And the fridge! It's filled with food! It's like a supermarket! I tell you, Dan, if you ever need a house-mate, just ring me up and I'll be straight over, shifting in. This place is great.'

Daniel's eyes were jumping from Flynn, buzzing like a bee in his face, to Chopper, who was rumbling in the throat, to the toolbox on the floor, its lid yawning open and the Ramset lying inside. He was perspiring and both his hands had fallen limply forward. Flynn paused and sighed. Turning to Sasha he said, 'Let me do it. I can't stand a man who arranges his clothes according to colour.'

Sasha smiled, and shook his head. He laid the baseball bat on the floor and lifted the gun from its place. 'This is a Ramset gun, Daniel,' he said. 'Do you know what it does?'

'No,' Daniel peeped.

'It uses an explosive charge to punch a nail into . . . well, into just about anything it wants to. The charges come in different strengths –

low, medium, strong, especially strong, you get the picture. When I heard what you've been doing to Alexandra, do you know what I said? I said, I'm gonna nail that bastard to the wall. And now I'm going to. The question that remains is, which hand first?'

'God,' Daniel breathed, 'don't. Don't. I swear, I won't tell the police if you just leave now, leave me alone – '

'You won't be telling the police, regardless of when we leave. Because if you do, some of our friends will be very upset. I think they'd hunt for you until they found you, and then I think you'd regret being born. So let's do this now, and get it over with, and get on with our lives, shall we?'

'Please – ' The man glanced at me. 'Please – '

'Which hand, Daniel?' Sasha repeated woodenly. Daniel looked away from me. His lips tremored, his knees sagged. Then he pissed himself. The piss first blackened a patch of his boxer shorts and then streamed down his right leg, its path guided by the hairiness of the skin. Flynn jumped from the puddle as it spread over the floorboards. 'Yeek,' he said. Sasha, Hastings and Andy looked from the wetness, to the man. Sasha decided, 'The right, I think.'

Daniel screamed. I had never heard a man scream before. It was surprisingly high-pitched. He screamed and thrashed his head from side to side and began to bellow, 'No, no, no – '

Sasha stepped forward, flattened the man's hand to the wall, brought the Ramset up and pulled the trigger. The noise of the explosion found shape in the arc of blood that shot from the place of impalement. Chopper roared, Sasha stepped back and the man pitched forward: instead of the nail bringing him up like a dog on a chain, Daniel flopped all the way to the floor. The nail had gone straight through the flesh and buried itself in the bricks. Sasha seemed impressed. 'Well,' he remarked, 'what do you know.'

I turned and walked out then, down the hall and through the front door, shutting it on the noise behind me. From the street you couldn't hear a thing. I tore the scarf from my face and the hat from my head, leaned into the garden and gagged, spitting up a rancid splatter of drool. I huddled into the steps, chest heaving, tears stinging my eyes. I wanted to be gone, but I didn't know where I was, and I yelled to the stranger who was still leaning against the fence. 'Where am I?' I yelled. 'Where am I?'

He didn't move a muscle: he looked at me like a cat would, unlikely to help even if it understood the request, a gaze cold and flat as concrete. I wiped my face, stood up carefully, and started to walk. The stranger watched me as I went. I tilted my head to look at the sky, and its stars were muted by the lights of the city.

It was a warm night, and windy; in a week it would be Christmas. I hadn't bought Andy a present, and now I wouldn't have to.

When they came out I was there, waiting. The toolbox was closed and Sasha had blood on his hands. We got in the cars and drove away and, before we rounded the first corner, I looked back to see the stranger still standing beside the fence, faithfully guarding the scene.

In the car I listened to them talk, but said nothing myself. I got Flynn to let me off at my house.

I never went back to the bungalow. Flynn invited me once or twice but I didn't go, and after that he stopped asking. I expected to cross paths with Andy when the new university year started but I didn't see him and later I heard that he'd dropped out of his course. Sasha I never heard from or about. I know it didn't have to be that way.

My pride was a titbit of a thing, easily swallowed. I could have gone back, steadfastly refusing to acknowledge that anything unusual had happened. Sasha may even have respected such gall. Treachery was something they understood; they depended on it; Andy, I'm sure, would have overlooked it. Elsbeth would have laughed at it, and Flynn would have lived with it. I could have pleaded my guiltlessness to Alexandra and she'd never have seen through my lies. With time, I would have wormed my way back in. I may even have found myself on steadier ground, for my edges had been roughened; I had been blooded. But that's not what happened; I went home.

I didn't want to be someone to whom nothing mattered. I didn't want to become someone who could hurt another and find it funny. I did not want to go through life seeing danger and enemies everywhere. I did not want to live on the lookout for a crack I could squeeze through to my own advantage, to the disadvantage of others. I didn't want to prey on weakness and innocence for the rest of my life. I wanted to be like them, but I wanted them to be more like me. So, I didn't go back.

My life is ordered now, flattened, peaceful. I visit Cassy and I help my mother around the house. I've stuck with my course and I'm doing an honours degree now. I attend to my work conscientiously and I'll get my thesis in on time. I am so ordinary. And, perhaps because this is the way things are, I miss them sometimes.

I have kept the jewellery Andy gave me, and the bits and pieces I was given for my part in their escapades. I have kept the soft toy Flynn stole for me and Alexandra's gift of a nut-brown bowl. I have kept, too, the things they taught me: don't forget the gloves, don't believe the police, right and wrong are funny things, chameleons.

I look for them on trains, at bars, standing on the kerb waiting for the traffic lights to change. It seems right that I never catch a glimpse of them. They're free to fly like birds through my memory, Sasha, Flynn, Andy, Hastings and Elsbeth, all of them far off and fragile as scraps of imagination. I don't know what I'd do if I actually saw them. Probably run.

This room is filled with smoke, and I am feeling tired. I can't yawn, it would look like I am bored. And maybe I am, a little: maybe everyone finds their own life boring. That night with the Ramset – I didn't find it interesting. I thought it was wrong – we went about it wrong. I said as much to Sasha, before the thing even happened, but he wasn't in the mood to listen to me. Send someone else, I told him, don't do this yourself. You risk being recognised. There's no need for four guys – two is enough. Get two guys that nobody knows and in the meantime you go to the pub and let everyone see you there, or watch television with your mother. But he wasn't listening. So I washed my hands of it, went along and made the best of it. I couldn't refuse to help him, even if I thought he was doing everything wrong. So now there's loose ends everywhere, and loose ends are only ever the result of bad planning. Sasha is stupid sometimes.

I'm angry at him anyway, for other things he's done. Sometimes I think I don't even know him; I don't think I should trust him. I don't like it when I'm angry with him, I try to push it down. Because I want to be here tomorrow.

Also, he needs me to be here tomorrow. Also, he knows he does.

It makes our friendship sound uneasy, but that's not how it is. Sasha Johns and I, we're as thick as thieves. We've only got each other to rely on. He thinks he has others, but I think he does not. So, while Alex drags him over the coals and back again, I look out the window and weave loose ends together in my head, until I've made a hammock that lifts both of us clean off the ground.

'If you had talked to me,' Sasha is saying, 'it would never have happened.'

'I didn't talk to you because I knew what *would* happen,' Alexandra cries. 'I knew you would do something idiotic!'

Kate says, 'I'm *glad* they did it. I'm *proud* of them. I think he got what he deserved.'

Alex shakes her head. 'No,' she says, 'no. *No one* deserves to have four masked guys break into his house and do what they did to him.'

Kate looks her in the eye. 'Daniel hurt you,' she says. 'He hit you and hurt you and made you frightened, and he did it time and time again. Think about that, Alexandra. Think about it, and tell me he didn't deserve it.'

They peer at Alexandra, but I shade my face with my hand. I want to tell them to shut up, to let me think. Kate is noisy:

everything she says, she seems to say at the top of her voice. When Alex doesn't answer immediately she says, 'You see.' To Sasha she says, 'If you had asked me, I would have come with you. I would have *helped*.'

'You still can,' I say slowly. The three of them look at me. I look at Sasha. 'Put the Ramset in the river,' I tell him.

'Why? It can't be traced to us.'

'Get rid of it.' It's dangerous to be found with a thing like that. He knows, and nods reluctantly.

'Tell Hastings to keep Chopper at home.' Sasha nods to this, too: the dog is easy to identify. I consider the burning end of my cigarette, thinking.

'I'm worried about Louie,' he says abruptly.

'Why?' I ask. 'You never were before.'

He looks sour. 'She'll be pissed off at us.'

'Not at *us*,' I say. He knows what I mean, and there's no pleasure in reminding him, 'She won't talk. She was there too, remember.'

He smiles. 'That leaves us. Where were we, that night?'

I stare at him: for a second I feel like punching him. I can't believe he's so into this, I can't believe he can still be bothered.

'Elsbeth will back up Hastings,' I say. 'Andy's housemates will say he was at home.'

'What about you and me? Huh?'

'I'll give you an alibi, Sasha,' says Kate. 'Say you were with me.'

Sasha looks her up and down; they give each other a smile that they think we don't see. Then they stare at me. For a minute the room is quiet and we hear the tick of Alexandra's watch. I'm used to taking care of myself and I'm not worried, but I know I look like the last kid picked for a team.

'Say you were with me, Flynn,' Alexandra says quietly.

I look at her. 'You don't have to do that.'

'I will, anyway,' she says. I'm not flattered, because I know she doesn't mean it like that: she means she has seen her other choices and seen that they are few, and knows that choosing one of them means going against us – and that's not what she's decided to do. It's not something that she can do, and have anything left to show for it. I feel sorry for her.

There's not much to say, after that. We can go.

We stand up and stretch our arms and legs and Jemima does the same, her body a golden curl. Someone mentions dinner and invites me to it but I say I should be getting home. We walk down the stairs to the garden, where the sprinklers are whipping droplets across the lawn, and from there we go our different ways. Driving home, I remember I've left my cigarettes at Sasha's place, and swear: tomorrow, there'll be nothing left for me but a crumpled empty pack.

About the Author

Sonya Hartnett was born in Melbourne in 1968 and is the author of several novels, having had her first, *Trouble All the Way*, published at the age of fifteen. Her titles published by Penguin include *Wilful Blue* (1994), *Sleeping Dogs* (1995), *The Devil Latch* (1996), *Black Foxes* (1996) and *Princes* (1997).

Wilful Blue, for which Hartnett received a writer's fellowship from the Literature Board of the Australia Council in 1992, was awarded the 1996 Ena Noël Award (International Board on Books for Young People).

Sleeping Dogs was the winner of the Sheaffer Pen Prize for Young Adult Fiction in the 1996 Victorian Premier's Awards, was an Honour Book in the 1996 Children's Book Council Book of the Year Awards (Older Readers), received the 1996 Kathleen Mitchell Award, and was shortlisted for the 1996 NSW Premier's Literary Award.

Also by Sonya Hartnett

WILFUL BLUE

Winner of the 1996 Ena Noël Award, this haunting novel explores the intertwined nature of talent and pain, and the mysterious and enduring bonds of friendship, love and memory.

SLEEPING DOGS

This critically acclaimed, multi-award-winning novel established Hartnett at the forefront of young adult writing in Australia.

Robert Cormier wrote:
'Sonya Hartnett has truly pushed the boundaries of YA literature to their outer edges and perhaps beyond, proving that new frontiers are always possible. We should be grateful to her for taking us there, even as we shudder at the terrible truths of her vision.'

THE DEVIL LATCH

'A triumphant marriage of style, plot and characterisation. From its creepy beginning to its chilling climax, The Devil Latch *maintains a tight grip.'*

Stephen Matthews,
the *Canberra Times*

PRINCES

In a dilapidated mansion overrun by rats, Ravel and Indigo Kesby are at war. In this house, there's no such thing as brotherly love.